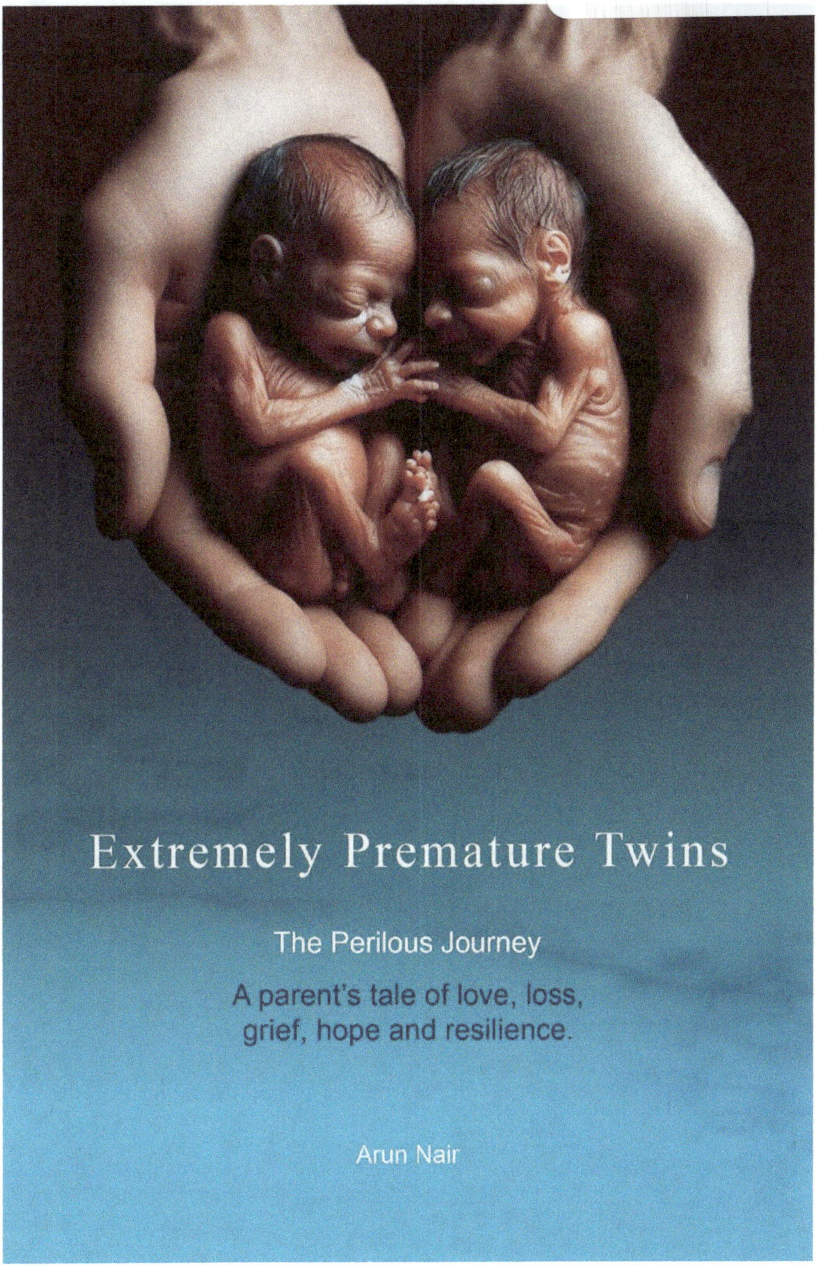

Extremely Premature Twins

The Perilous Journey

A parent's tale of love, loss,
grief, hope and resilience.

Arun Nair

Dedicated to the families of babies who have endured

NewBorn Intensive Care and to the Neonatal Nursing staff,

Nurse Practitioners, other support staff and Medical colleagues

who toil day and night to save and give better life to babies and

their families.

Table of Contents

Acknowledgments

I wish to thank my family, who helped me bring this book to conclusion with their immense patience and encouragement. A special acknowledgment goes to my talented daughter, Nandini Nair, for her exceptional efforts in designing the cover and setting up the book's format.

Special thanks to Dr Eleanor Carmichael, an accomplished Developmental Paediatrician and my ex-colleague at work. Dr Carmichael was the recipient of the Queen's Service Medal in 2009 for Services to the community. She not only wrote the foreword for this book but also gave me valuable advice regarding the parental perspective from her experience of looking after her own extremely premature twins. I owe Dr. Carmichael immensely for carefully going over the manuscript to make it readable to parents, healthcare workers and the general reader.

Foreword

I am very pleased to offer a welcome to those who come to this book.

As a pediatrician and a parent of 27-week twins, I and my family walked the newborn unit pathway happily without the major potholes and loss described here.

Arun, based on his vast experience, has laid out the important healthcare activities and steps made by healthcarers to get the best outcome for extremely premature infants and their families.

As you prepare to work with and care for these fragile families, use this book to understand what is happening and, if possible, to anticipate complications before they occur.

On behalf of your babies and their future well-being, thank you for your interest.

— Dr Eleanor Carmichael

Introduction

"Forewarned, forearmed; to be prepared is half the victory."
—Miguel de Cervantes

As a retired Neonatal Paediatrician with over four decades of experience, I embarked on this literary journey driven by a profound observation—the stark disconnects between parental expectations and the harsh realities faced when an extremely premature baby enters the world unexpectedly. The birth of a baby should be the most joyous occasion for a family, but the potential for things to go awry is real, and oftentimes, it comes as a rude shock. Despite the comprehensive information provided by healthcare professionals in such situations, parents often find themselves unprepared and emotionally overwhelmed.

"Extremely Premature Twins: The Perilous Journey & A Parents' Tale of Love, Loss, Grief, Hope and Resilience" derives its title from the poignant dilemmas parents encounter during the critical period preceding their baby's birth and throughout their journey in the Newborn Intensive Care Unit (NICU). In exercising my creative freedom as a writer, I've crafted a family story to draw readers into the emotional journey of parents with prematurely born babies. The initial backgrounds of the main characters are purely imaginative, yet the medical scenarios presented in this book draw inspiration from the experiences of a real couple's extremely premature twins. However, this narrative is not a direct account of their lives. The medical aspects depicted are firmly grounded in the numerous cases I've encountered throughout my career. The healthcare professionals you will encounter within these pages are real—familiar to my ex-colleagues and patients—but their identities remain veiled by their names being changed to protect their privacy.

The purpose of this book is twofold: to illuminate the struggles, dilemmas, and raw emotions experienced by parents and healthcare professionals alike and to unveil the intricate saga of families navigating the complexities of premature birth. It provides an intimate glimpse into the emotional rollercoaster faced not only by parents but also by the dedicated healthcare providers who tirelessly care for these fragile infants during their precarious early days. It is important to mention upfront that most families would have extraordinary capabilities to cope with extreme situations and readjust their lives in the face of disasters when forewarned, hence this book.

The book may come as a bit technical to non-medical people and parents, but bear with me. The purpose is to introduce and help anticipate the various issues that can come up during intensive care in the newborn unit. In my effort to engage non-medical readers, I have tried to explain complex medical issues in accessible language, as far as possible, at the same time ensuring that the narrative remains scientifically accurate. While firmly grounded in the specialized field of neonatal/perinatal medicine, this book hopefully aspires to resonate with a broader audience—a testament to the universal themes of resilience, hope, and the human spirit.

The field of perinatal medicine, as ancient as humanity itself, has witnessed remarkable advancements over the past half-century. I have included some important and interesting historical facts from the last few decades that have shaped the current neonatal/perinatal practice. These breakthroughs have enabled a spectacular increase in the survival of extremely premature babies in recent times - miraculous achievements. Yet, our journey does not end with survival alone; it extends to enhancing the quality of life for these resilient survivors and their families. The medical community remains steadfast in its pursuit of progress.

Lastly, I extend my heartfelt gratitude to the families and fellow professionals who have shaped my career. As I reflect upon my time, even in retirement, I remain connected to the exciting developments in perinatal research. Together, we strive to alleviate the human suffering that accompanies illness

— *Arun Nair*

Saving the Twins

To save David's life, Samson and David had to be delivered fifteen weeks early, because of David's perilously worsening condition in the womb. Rosy and Robert Tam, first-time parents, faced the agonizing recommendation from the medical team and agreed to the early delivery. This decision meant both boys would face the harsh realities of extreme prematurity. The weight of this choice was immense, and they had no idea how profoundly it would alter their lives forever.

Worldwide, about ten percent of babies are born prematurely. Normal human pregnancy should last forty weeks. When the babies are born earlier than thirty-seven completed weeks gestational age (GA), they are called preterm or premature. There are sub-categories of preterm birth, based on GA: Extremely Preterm (less than 28 weeks), very preterm (28 to less than 32 weeks), and moderate to late preterm (32 to 37 weeks).

There are many known reasons for premature birth. Multiple pregnancies like twins and triplets have a higher tendency to be delivered early. Then, there are reasons related to mothers' illnesses medically, physically, and/or emotionally. There are also reasons, such as babies being abnormal. With the progress in time, there has been an increase due to medical interventions during pregnancy for either mother's or baby's sake. However, by and large, in a substantial proportion of pregnancies, the cause would remain elusive. It just happens; that is how nature dictates terms.

The problem with being born prematurely is that the babies are then not fully developed for independent existence. The more premature they are, the more immature their organ systems become.

While in the womb, the babies are provided nutrition and oxygen through an organ called the placenta.

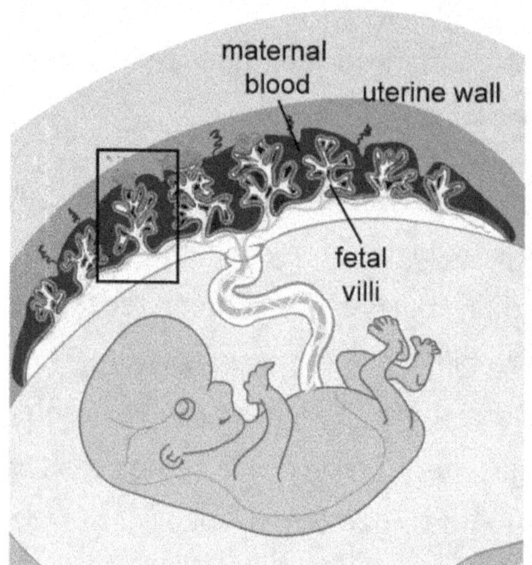

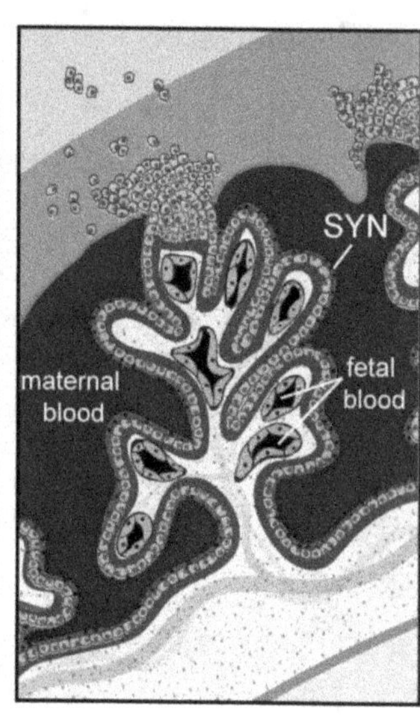

The placenta is like a connecting plate that attaches the baby to the inner wall of the womb. The two surfaces of the plate have different architectures. The one on the mother's side has large channels of the baby's blood vessels interwoven with channels of blood from the mother. These channels are separated by membranes through which oxygen and nutrition can easily diffuse under normal circumstances. While on the other side, the baby's channels coalesce into three major blood vessels, which help take nutrition and oxygen that diffuse from the mother into the baby and bring back carbon dioxide and other waste products from the baby to be disposed of by the mother. The life of a growing baby (fetus) could be in danger if the functioning of the placenta and the blood vessels traversing through it is impaired in any which way.

In the case of multiple pregnancies, each baby would have its own blood vessels draining into it from the placenta. The placenta itself may be an independent unit, or it could be a single unit. In the case of single units, there is a danger that the blood vessels of one baby are intermingling with the other's. In such a situation, the blood could be unevenly distributed, one getting more and the other less, thus compromising the lives of both babies. This sort of situation occurs only in identical twins, as in the case of Samson and David. Here, David's blood was preferentially draining away from him into Samson. The obstetricians had felt that David was more compromised than Samson and he was in imminent danger of demise. There were several dilemmas- what are the chances of David surviving if delivered at that point in pregnancy? What about Samuel's chances for survival, then? Can we selectively deliver only David, alive or dead? What about leaving David inside but dead and allowing Samuel to grow? It is not about survival alone; it is about survival without complications – intact survival.

And so, in the quiet of that delivery room, Rosy and Robert Tam grappled with life's most profound questions. The placenta—the silent sentinel—held their twins' destinies in its intricate channels. For Samson and David, the delicate balance between maternal and foetal blood flow became a lifeline—a fragile thread connecting them to existence. And as the monitors blinked, measuring heartbeats and breaths, the world held its breath too, waiting to witness the resilience of life—woven together by the placenta's silent magic. Samson and David's story epitomizes the delicate balance between life and uncertainty. Their premature arrival forever altered the Tams' lives, leaving them to navigate the uncharted waters of parenthood.

Science tells us that the chances for intact survival increase with every increase in the weeks that the fetus lives in the womb till they are forty weeks. Modern technology has the potential to save very premature babies, as young as twenty-two to twenty-four weeks. The question, however, is not about survival alone; it is about the quality of survival. More and more high-risk and smaller and smaller babies are now surviving the world over. There is an increasing number of data now being published looking at the long-term outcome. While the quality of life of newer cohorts is continually improving thanks to better and evidence-based practices, the general feeling still is that on a population basis, the more premature the baby is at birth, the more are the chances for them to suffer from developmental problems, medical illnesses, and other psychosocial morbidities.

Rosy & Robert

In 2009, amidst the bustling cafeteria of Auckland Medical School, fate brought together Rosy Lim and Robert Tam. This chance encounter was destined to shape their lives in unimaginable ways.

Rosy, a third-year medical student, was the only child of Chinese immigrants from Zhejiang province. Born in New Zealand to parents in their late thirties, her father, Joseph Lim, was an engineer, and her mother, Mary Lim, was a librarian. Despite their comfortable life, they sought a better future abroad, moving to New Zealand in the early eighties. Mary, fluent in English and a graduate of Zhejiang University, had met Joseph, an ambitious engineer from a wealthy family, through their shared neighborhood. Their bond grew from mutual respect and a shared thirst for knowledge. They immigrated to New Zealand and welcomed Rosy into the world at Greenlane Maternity Hospital in 1986.

Rosy excelled both academically and artistically, guided by her mother's encouragement towards a career in science despite her own passion for the arts. Her outstanding academic performance secured her a spot at Auckland Medical School, where she carried the legacy of her parents' sacrifices and dreams.

Robert, originally from South Korea, was born to technocrat parents, with his father, Kwan Tam, in the IT sector and his mother, Hei Young, working at South Korean Telephones. After his father's transfer to Auckland, Robert stayed back with his grandparents in South Korea until finishing primary school. Adjusting to life in New Zealand was challenging for Robert, but his interest in science and biology remained steadfast. He excelled at Auckland Grammar School and easily secured admission to medical school, joining three years before Rosy.

Robert, intense and serious, rarely smiled, contrasting sharply with Rosy's cheerful and popular demeanor. Drawn to Robert's looks and stature at the school, Rosy would often see him alone, engrossed in his medical journals. One day, she mustered the courage to sit opposite him and initiate a conversation. Despite his initial reticence, Robert gradually warmed up to her presence. Their conversations began with intellectual and medical topics but soon expanded to more personal discussions.

As their relationship developed, Robert began opening up about his life. He shared stories of his upbringing, his rebellion against his father's career plans for him, and his desire to become a cardiologist—fueled by the loss of his beloved grandmother to a heart attack. His serious demeanor masked a deep-seated passion and sensitivity that Rosy slowly uncovered.

Their relationship deepened over time, marked by conversations that bridged their diverse backgrounds and personalities. Through Rosy's persistence and Robert's growing trust, they discovered a profound connection that balanced seriousness with charm and intellect with empathy. As time passed, Rosy and Robert grew closer. In the summer of 2002, Robert graduated with distinction in medicine. Rosy and her family attended the ceremony, fully aware of her relationship with Robert. They had met him six months earlier during her mid-semester break. Despite their initial apprehensions about his nationality, they were impressed by his achievements and demeanor, viewing him as a suitable match for their daughter.

Robert, however, had not openly expressed his feelings for Rosy. While Rosy hoped he would propose soon, Robert's parents' presence at the ceremony complicated matters. Rosy and her parents were disappointed when Robert didn't introduce them to his parents. Her parents remained silent on the way home, with her mother eventually breaking down, unable to bear the thought of her daughter being ignored.

Robert had already moved to Hawkes Bay for his internship before the official graduation ceremony and promptly returned after the event. His calls to Rosy became less frequent, which she initially attributed to his busy schedule. However, she noticed it was always her who reached out, and she began to worry about losing him. This started to affect her mood and concentration, with her friends noticing her change.

Feeling the distance grow, Rosy decided to visit Robert unannounced in Hawkes Bay to reassess his feelings. Meanwhile, Robert was dealing with his own struggles. He had invited his parents to the ceremony, hoping they wouldn't attend. However, they eagerly accepted, unaware of Robert's strained relationship with them. His father, now a prominent figure at Samsung, had long forgiven Robert for not following in his footsteps and was proud of his son's achievements.

Robert's last meaningful conversation with his mother had ended acrimoniously. He had tested her reaction to his potential marriage to Rosy by discussing his admiration for independent women and criticizing the submissive nature of women back home. This led to a heated argument, leaving their relationship strained.

His parents had planned to introduce Robert to Miss Lily Chang, the daughter of a visiting business tycoon from South Korea. They brought the family along uninvited to the ceremony and whisked Robert away for dinner, preventing him from meeting Rosy's family. This upset Robert, and he chose not to discuss the night's events with Rosy, becoming more reclusive and immersing himself in work.

When Rosy turned up that morning at Hawkes Bay Hospital, Robert was indeed surprised. He had been in an irritable mood since a long and difficult night at the ED, packing up to go back to his room for some rest. Rosy noted his discomfiture but couldn't fathom what was upsetting him. Not a doctor yet, she didn't realize how draining and difficult a night at the ED could be. She was more concerned that he might be hiding something from her.

They walked back to Robert's room in silence. The room was dingy and unkempt, with books strewn everywhere, unwashed dishes in the sink, and a musty odor from lack of circulation. It was hardly a place for a decent conversation, let alone a romantic one. Rosy, tired from the all-night bus trip, and Robert, exhausted from his shift, exchanged brief pleasantries and had a modest breakfast before drifting off to sleep.

When they woke up in the late afternoon, Robert's head had cleared, and he realized what was going on. He had completely failed to read Rosy's mind. It didn't take much talking from Rosy before Robert realized how close he was to losing her. Rosy, on the other hand, was relieved that Robert was just being himself. It took her a while to get Robert to tell his side of the story. Tears started rolling from her eyes, and Robert, touched by her tenderness, took her in his arms, kissed her, and made love to her. Not long after, he mustered the courage to propose to her.

The wedding took place a year later. Rosy was in her penultimate year at medical school, and Robert had moved to Hamilton to work as a senior house officer at Waikato Hospital. The year leading up to the wedding was eventful. Rosy's family was very happy, but Robert had some work to do with his parents.

When Robert announced his decision to marry Rosy, his parents were shocked. He had not told them until he finished his internship at Hawkes Bay. He expected drama, considering their conservative outlook, but their reaction was harsher than he anticipated. His father was particularly upset, not so much about Rosy's Chinese origin but about her family's middle-class status. His mother, with whom he had not had a decent conversation for months, stopped talking to him altogether.

It hurt Robert that his parents were more concerned with their social status than his happiness. He stopped visiting them or making the customary weekend calls. He would have completely cut them off if Rosy hadn't insisted on re-establishing links and seeking their blessings for the wedding. Rosy had not met his family yet, but she knew in her heart that if she could meet his mother, things would turn around.

Rosy had some South Korean friends at medical school and planned to mingle with them more to understand their way of life. She was confident that if she managed to meet Robert's mother, she could use her charm to soften her attitude. Luckily, one of her South Korean friends' family attended the same church as Robert's family. Rosy knew from Robert about his mother's preoccupation with religious rituals.

Rosy was active at her local church, helping raise funds for charity and other functions. She loved meeting people and enjoyed the atmosphere, playing the piano, and occasionally leading the choir.

As Christmas approached, Rosy volunteered to play the piano for the church's Christmas activities, where Robert's mother was organizing a music show. Through regular interactions during practice sessions, Rosy found Robert's mother to be warm and likable, contrary to Robert's portrayal. When she finally revealed her identity as a medical student, Robert's mother asked if she knew her son. Emotionally overwhelmed, Rosy couldn't speak, but Robert's mother soon pieced together the truth. Mixed emotions of anger, sympathy, and joy washed over her, and she embraced Rosy, both crying in each other's arms.

The Wedding

The parents met at the church two weeks before Christmas. To everyone's relief, it was a pleasant meeting. Both Robert and Rosy had kept away. The wedding date was fixed for the eve of New Year as per Robert's wishes.

The wedding was a simple affair. Robert would not allow anyone other than the immediate family to be present at the church. Rosy and the rest of the family members had relented but on the promise from Robert that a more elaborate reception could be arranged at a later date.

The next few months were particularly difficult for the couple, with Robert being at Waikato and Rosy busy with her final year at the med school in Auckland. Robert had moved on from Hawkes Bay to Waikato Hospital for further training. Rosy could not wait to join him at Waikato. They met every weekend till, finally, Rosy finished her exams and moved over towards the end of what looked like a long, harsh winter. Rosy managed to get her internship at Waikato Hospital. By the time she commenced her rotation, Robert had finished his first year of house officer runs.

The wedding reception was arranged at the picturesque Vineyard Resort Hotel at Hawkes Bay. Robert had visited this place many times during his stay in Hawkes Bay. Surrounded by hills and nestled deep in the vineyard country, this was the ideal setting for any function of this sort. Robert had taken Rosy there after his proposal on the morning after she had sprung the surprise visit on him. He had indeed thought about this place for the wedding, although he had never mentioned it to Rosy.

The resort hotel had an ambiance of its own. There was a beautiful manmade lake in its foreground. The green lawn around the lake stretching from the lake to the hotel was the makeshift reception area. It was already spring, and the scenery around was picture-perfect that evening. Robert looked handsome in his tuxedo and bow tie. Rosy was beautiful in her own way. The white flowing bride's gown added further to her radiant charm. The guest list was small; only close friends and a select few of either family's relatives were invited. The guests were all dressed to the hilt. The ladies were in their best dresses, and the men were all suited and booted. There were short speeches from the parents of the bride and the groom followed by an exchange of vows once again by the now not-so-newlyweds. It was a joyous occasion, and after raising a toast to the couple, everyone moved into the dining area. What followed was amazing; a light rain broke out from nowhere. It was as if the Gods from heaven had decided to bless the couple. The food and wine were sumptuous; everyone had a great time.

The days and months passed by thereafter without any notable events in their personal life. Both Rosy and Robert were busy working towards their careers. Robert had cleared his membership exam and went about his rotations as a registrar in internal medicine. Rosy completed her house officership and was selected for training in radiology. Although they were both based in Waikato and stayed under the same roof as husband and wife, there were days when their careers took over their personal lives.

They had not taken a holiday in a long time. It had been almost two years since their wedding. One fine day, Rosy decided that it was time to take some time off. Robert was in the crucial stage of preparations for his membership examination when they married. Therefore, the honeymoon trip was postponed, but Robert had promised her that once he wass through his examination, they could take a trip abroad. Rosy had never forgotten that, but she herself got carried away by her desire to get into training in radiology. Now that they both were relatively settled in their career path, she thought it was time to broach the topic with Robert. To her pleasant surprise, Robert readily agreed. They decided that they should take a few months off and travel the world. They both were particularly interested in visiting their respective countries of origin. So, one fine day, they packed up their bags and set out.

The Honeymoon

This was the first time for Rosy to leave New Zealand. Her parents had visited their homeland in China many times but had never taken Rosy along. She was excited. She was looking forward to visiting her parent's town and meeting with her extended family. She had heard so many stories from her parents about their lives and the hardships they faced. She was also aware that the landscape and the society had changed vastly from the time her parents had left the shores. She was prepared to experience the cultural difference but was least prepared for the lack of freedom that was second nature to her in New Zealand. The moment they landed at Shanghai airport, they could sense the feeling of being watched. The crowd was overwhelming, and the long queues at the counters were an entirely new experience. She had no problem communicating in the native language, though, as she was proficient; she had always talked to her parents in Cantonese. It did not matter to Robert. He was, as usual, quiet, and with Rosy around, he did not have to speak much. They spend a couple of weeks going around the main cities of Shanghai and Beijing before venturing inland.

The rural areas were refreshingly different from the megacities. For a country portrayed by the media as poor, she was particularly impressed by the opulence in the cities, but she knew that the true nature of the country would be revealed when she visited her parent's hometown in Zhejiang.

The place was as she had imagined from her parent's description. She was surprised at how little had changed in the long years since her parents had migrated. She met with her uncles and aunts. Her maternal grandmother was still alive. She looked old and fragile but still had the steely determination in her eyes reminiscent of her own mother. Her grandma and the rest of the relatives were overwhelmed with joy at seeing her and Robert. She had brought along gifts, which were particularly picked up by her mother for each member of the family. They stayed for a few days before heading to South Korea.

Robert's family lived in the metropolis of Seoul. He had returned on a regular basis when he was young, but after joining Medical School, this was his first visit. He had no likes or dislikes about the city. After the death of his grandmother, he did not have enough time to bond with the rest of his extended family. Being a loner by nature, he never ventured to forge any relationship. Rosy's arrival, however, changed the scene. She mingled with everyone and soon realized that Robert had many cousins. She became friends with everyone and had a rollicking time. They visited all the important places and generally had a good time. While there, the time passed very fast, and before they could gather their thoughts, they were on their way back home.

The Pregnancy

Upon returning home, they quickly got back into their routines. The work at the hospital kept them busy. It was the beginning of winter by the time they returned, not the best of times for good health or mood, but neither of them was particularly affected until Rosy realized that she had missed her periods. It was one of those weekends when she could sit down and ponder. Both had extended periods of calls at work involving the weekends and had not managed to be at home together for a while. Life was getting too hectic, and they were looking forward to this weekend. This weekend, they had planned to sit down and reorganize their lives. Robert had gone to procure the weekly purchases. The realization that she may be pregnant came as a whiff of pleasant tidings. All of a sudden she felt a warmth flow through her veins, and a sense of happiness and fulfillment, emotions she had never experienced before, overcame her. She could not wait for Robert to return. She immediately phoned Robert and asked him to drop everything and head back home. She would not tell him what or why. From her tone, he did realize that she was extremely happy but could not fathom why.

He had not seen her so bubbly in a long time and was happy himself. He kept thinking of all the possible reasons as he drove back home. Was it the news of her first paper being accepted for publication? No, that will not make her so happy. He wondered if his in-laws were in town. He did not have a particularly friendly relationship, so that could not be the reason. What about his mother landing up unannounced? Over the years, Rosy and his mum had gotten along very well, but he was unsure if that could make Rosy so happy, considering that he would not be comfortable with his mom being around. So, what is it? By the time he reached home, Rosy had completely rearranged the furniture. There were fresh flowers in the pot; the old withered flowers had not been changed since they returned from their trip abroad. There was soothing music and a waft of air with the fragrance of freshly cooked Jajangmyeon. His favorite Chinese dish greeted him as he opened the door, and there she was, standing all dressed up with that look of 'Guess what?' He knew instantly that something special had happened since he left in the morning, but as was his nature, he revealed no emotions. It did not take long before Rosy blurted out that they were going to be parents soon. Robert froze in his stands. He could not figure out what had hit him. This was never in his scheme of things. Rosy could not contain her happiness; she kept singing and dancing all around him. It took a while before Robert spoke. In his very careful demeanor, he checked if she was sure and if they were ready. After all, they were still in training; there were a lot of hard choices to make. The examinations were just a few months away for him and were his prime concern till now. Rosy had just entered training; she had a few more years to go. Suddenly, her priorities changed; she was ready to be a mother.

It took a while for Robert to feel comfortable, but Rosy was so happy he refrained from showing his discomfort. A myriad of thoughts kept swirling in his head. He was confused; he did not know what to think or do, whether to be happy or concerned; he could not believe that he was having mixed emotions. However, he kept his emotions under check for days on end, all the time keeping up a positive front in the presence of Rosy. Eventually, as time passed by, he started looking forward to fatherhood and the responsibility that it entails.

Rosy suggested that they should be seeing a General Practitioner (GP) soon. Until then, they had not felt the need to register with a GP. In New Zealand, like many developed countries, the first point of contact for medical reasons is the GP. The obstetric care is, however, largely driven by midwives, at least for low-risk pregnancies. Rosy contacted the nearby Hamilton East Medical Centre for registration and made an appointment to visit their GP, Dr Baba Shankar. They could visit the centre the next Saturday when both Robert and she were off from work at the hospital. There was an expectant excitement. Dr Shankar's office was a warm and welcoming room. The walls were well adorned with certificates from India, UK, and New Zealand. Dr Shankar had apparently trained as an obstetrician from south India. He later moved to the United Kingdom and trained again, but on arrival in New Zealand, he was asked to retrain by the Medical Council. He instead decided to train as a general practitioner. Rosy and Robert were ushered into his office at the appointed time by the secretary at the practice. The fifteen-minute consultation allowed very little time for an exchange of niceties, but Dr Shankar, in his own charismatic fashion, made the couple comfortable. After cursory introductions, he went quickly through the process of consultation and ordered a pregnancy test. The result did not take long to come. The pregnancy was confirmed as Rosy expected. He then referred them to his favorite midwife colleague, Ms. Wilkinson. With this, the couple had got into the system, as they say.

The initial excitement soon became a distant memory. Rosy developed significant nausea and vomiting – hyperemesis gravidarum, which is not uncommon in early pregnancies. It was significant enough for her to need admission more than once for intravenous fluid administration. Along with this came some strange taste fetishes. Robert went out of the way to fulfill her desire to eat various food items. It was a tough period for both. However, realizing that it was only a temporary phase that would pass eventually, they carried on. Rosy's colleagues were kind enough to cover for her at work, and Robert was very understanding. Her parents had temporarily moved down to Hamilton for help. The first ultrasound test was scheduled in the coming weeks, and they were hopeful that by then, she would feel much better.

Weeks passed by, and her problems with nausea and vomiting started to abate, and the eventual day for the ultrasound arrived. Ms. Wilkinson referred them to the Hamilton Radiology Centre. Robert could not make it, but Rosy had her parents in. They were more than happy to accompany their daughter. Although Rosy was only in the early years of her training in radiology, the ultrasonologist, Dr. Pfizer, was familiar with Rosy through their interactions on the phone at work, with Rosy as a trainee radiologist. She was ushered in at the appointed time. Dr. Pfizer, herself a fully trained obstetrician with special expertise in feto-maternal medicine, had worked at the Waikato Hospital for several years before and was an experienced hand. Rosy recognized her from her earlier house officer run in the labor ward at the hospital. After the usual pleasantries were exchanged, Dr Pfizer went about the procedure. Rosy was very relaxed and was reflecting on life and the turn of events. She was pleasantly surprised when Dr. Pfizer exclaimed, "Good news, Rosy, you have twin boys. Aren't you excited?" Before she could react, she was shown the faint outlines of the two fetuses. Dr. Pfizer also mentioned that it looked like there was just one placenta, meaning they could be identical twins.

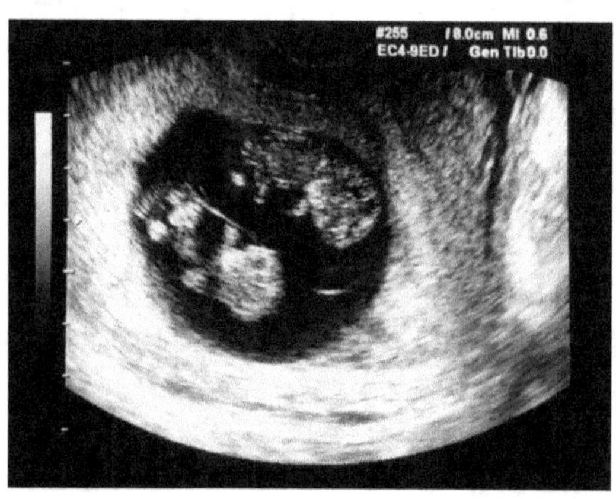

While her parents rejoiced at the exciting news of having twin grandchildren, Rosy was not so sure. Her training as a doctor and her runs in the obstetric and newborn unit reminded her of all the potential problems and complications that one can expect, and she was gripped with a sense of anxiety. She was also worried about how Robert would take it. However, it came as a relief to her later when Robert reacted not only positively but she could see him pleasantly drifting into a reverie of life with two kids growing together. He even suggested the names David and Samson for his unborn sons. She, therefore, refrained from reminding him of all her concerns and even quietly accepted the names suggested by Robert. Ms. Wilkinson, her midwife, called later that evening to organize a meeting to outline her plan of management from then on. Another ultrasound test was to be organized when Rosy reached 20 weeks gestation, called the anatomy scan. It was to assess if all the organ systems of David and Samson were developing and growing normally. The next few weeks passed by rather uneventfully. They were excited when Ms Wilkinson alerted them to the possibility of hearing their sons; heartbeats at about 16 to 18 weeks. Robert, being a cardiologist in training, wasted no time to start listening to their heartbeats every day. He jumped with joy when, one fine day, he thought he had heard what sounded like a fetal heartbeat. Rosy was amused to see his child-like enthusiasm and prayed to God for everything to go well. Both Rosy and Robert went about their life as trainee doctors, busy with work, learning, meetings, and calls, blissfully unaware of any problems that lay ahead till the appointed day for the ultrasound arrived. Robert was very keen this time to accompany Rosy; he had already applied for a day off from his work and was looking forward to seeing their sons' hearts beating on ultrasound. Rosy was nervous but did not let Robert know, seeing how excited he was.

The Anatomy Scan

On the day of the appointment, Rosy and Robert drove down, starting early in the morning. It is a little over an hour's drive up north to Auckland from Hamilton. The roads get congested as you enter the main city, which, like any other major metropolis in the Western world, is quite busy on a working day. About two-thirds of New Zealand's five million odd population live there. Most of the major sub-specialists of medicine live and work in Auckland, being the country's main tertiary care centre. The Feto-maternal medicine clinic is run by a group of highly specialized professionals. It is situated at the National Women's Hospital. Being the apex hospital, they get referrals from all over the country. Rosy and Robert arrived just before the appointed time, enough for them to have a cup of coffee at the cafeteria in the hospital foyer. They walked in to find the clinic buzzing with activity. There were at least a dozen pregnant women and their relatives waiting for their call. Rosy did not have to wait long before they were ushered in by the secretary with a pleasing smile, manning the table in the foyer. Rosy was nervous and was silently praying for everything to go fine, while Robert appeared rather relaxed. Rosy was relieved to see Mr. Fox, the most senior of the obstetricians & experienced fetal medicine specialist. Both Rosy and Robert had attended a few of his lectures during their medical school years at Auckland. Dr Fox was a charming old man with a pleasing personality. He made them both very comfortable after exchanging some pleasantries. He appeared happy to learn that both Rosy and Rob were graduates of Auckland Medical School and got about his business right away. Rob was keenly observing the ultrasound screen while Mr Fox went about the examination. Rosy focussed on his facial expression to pick up any indication of a problem, but there was none that she could decipher. She glanced occasionally towards Robert, who seemed completely immersed in admiring his twin son's images. Mr. Fox did say a few words as he got going about how the twins were active and oriented in the womb but became gradually quiet as he maneuvered the ultrasound probe on Rosy's abdomen. Once the examination was over, he called them both aside into the tiny office adjacent to the scan room. He took a deep breath before uttering what appeared to Rosy as nothing unusual when he said, "Look, the babies are sharing a single placenta," and then he waited for what looked like a long time while Rosy and Robert absorbed the information. Then, he explained to them what it means for their children in the womb. He tried to sound very positive and optimistic and told them that the babies were normal from the anatomy scan point but that there was a chance that the babies were sharing the blood and, therefore, it would be important to monitor their progress with a weekly scan to make sure that both David and Samson are growing well. Rosy and Rob had learned of the condition called intertwining in their obstetric house officer runs but did not make much of it. They both became anxious and wanted to know more but found Mr. Fox impatient to move on to his next patient. Therefore, realizing that there were other patients waiting to be scanned, they decided to leave the questioning for another day after they saw the final report.

Twin pregnancies occur at about a rate of one per eighty pregnancies. About two-thirds of them are usually non-identical or fraternal twins, and about a third are identical. Non-identical twins can run in families, but identical twins do not have a familial, heritable tendency. The non-identical twins arise from the fertilization of two ovum (eggs). They often have two different placental units, meaning they are independent of each other for supply of oxygen and nutrition. Identical twinning occurs when one single fertilized ovum divides to form two individual babies. Depending on when or how early the division occurs, one can have a range of outcomes leading to, in extremely rare circumstances, conjoined twins, where various parts of the body of the twins are joined together, with babies sharing organs. More commonly, though, the division occurs early enough to have two fully formed individual babies. However, depending upon the division, the babies may have individual placenta (the connecting unit to the uterus) or a single placenta. If it turns out to be a single placenta, called monochorionic in medical jargon, there develops the potential complication from intertwining, meaning sharing of blood supply. For reasons not very well understood, there is never a perfect balance in such a situation, with one twin getting more than the other and, at times, one twin getting overloaded at the expense of the other. Depending upon how severe this imbalance is, the life of both babies could be compromised in the womb. There are measures the feto-maternal experts could use to close some of the communicating channels if picked up early. However, there are limitations and risks involved in this procedure that could result in either premature births or the death of one or both twins. Sometimes, the discrepancy in the size of the twins is so large that nothing can be done other than delivering them early as they reach the viable gestational age, the age at which the prematurely born baby can be saved by the available resources in a particular setup. Most so-called developed or advanced nations currently have the necessary resources to look after babies born as early as 22 – 23 weeks. Irrespective of the complications listed, twin pregnancies, in general, have higher chances of ending in premature delivery; rarely do they reach the full-term gestation of nine months. Fortunately, a large majority of the twins, even when identical, go on to reach near-term gestation. Even so, being born prematurely at any gestational age would have its own challenges that may have long-lasting consequences for the babies and their immediate families going late into their adulthood. The earlier the babies are born, the more the expected problems involving survival and morbidities related to the immaturity of their organ systems alone; any complication on and above that would bring in additional challenges.

The return journey was anything but comfortable. Robert had gone even quieter than usual, and a thousand thoughts were arising in Rosy's mind. She tried to recollect what they had learned in medical school about intertwining and then quickly searched it on her mobile phone. While Robert kept a straight face and uttered very little, Rosy kept talking and reading aloud from the Google Scholar that she had downloaded just a few weeks ago on her iPhone.

The next few weeks were spent commuting to Auckland for scans and maternal-fetal medicine clinic visits. Both Rob and Rosy tried hard to keep themselves occupied with their training, but with every passing week, they got more anxious. In the fourth week, Dr Fox told them that David's growth was slowing down. He was increasingly getting deprived of blood, with the channels of blood showing a preference of flow into Samson. By then, the gestation had advanced beyond the period of viability, and they were given a choice of intervention to try selectively closing those channels. They were left to decide if they would take that advice considering the possibility of triggering the early onset of premature labor. They were told that the time is nearing when the window of opportunity to attempt the procedure may close down, and they may be left with either one or both of the babies dying in the womb, more likely David. It did not take long for them to make that decision. They decided to go ahead right away. Rosy was then admitted to the maternity ward overnight with a plan to go ahead with the procedure the next morning. Fortunately, the procedure went smoothly, Dr Fox was happy and positive about the outcome. She was then discharged following the mandatory period of observation with advice to come back the week after for a review. Rob and Rosy were quite relieved. They drove back to Hamilton with the hope that everything would be alright from then on. The next day, Rosy decided to stay back at home and rest while Rob got back to work.

Premature Labour

The next morning, Rosy started feeling a bit uncomfortable when she got up but did not let Rob be aware, hoping that she would feel better as the day went by. She could not relax, no matter what she tried. She spent some time playing the piano after breakfast, but her mind kept going back to the prospect of setting into labor at any moment. By that afternoon, she felt some pain, and it started getting more frequent with time. She was not sure if she should call Rob, so she called her mother instead, who came in to be with her. Her dad came along a few minutes later, and together, they decided that it would be better for her to call her midwife. Ms. Wilkinson had a brief chat with Rosy and decided that the pains that rosy was feeling sounded very much like the early onset of labor. She advised them to go straight to the Delivery Suite at Waikato Hospital and told them that she would call Dr. Pfizer and update her right away.

As she hung up the phone, Ms. Wilkinson's mind raced with thoughts. She had seen many cases of premature labor, each one bringing its own set of challenges and emotions. The balance between calm professionalism and deep empathy was a delicate dance she performed daily. She could not help but think about Rosy, a first-time mother, probably terrified and overwhelmed. Ms. Wilkinson's own experiences in the delivery room flashed through her mind—moments of triumph, relief, and sometimes sorrow.

She felt a rush of urgency, knowing how crucial every moment was for both Rosy and her baby. Her immediate concern was ensuring that Rosy received the best possible care without delay. As she prepared to head to the delivery suite herself, she took a deep breath, steeling herself for the tasks ahead. She knew that her calm demeanor and quick actions would set the tone for Rosy's experience. With one final check of her supplies, Ms. Wilkinson headed out, ready to provide the support and expertise that Rosy and her baby needed.

So, Rosy was taken to the hospital that afternoon by her parents. Before she left home, she called Rob, who said that he would meet her in the delivery suite. The triage nurse at the admission quickly prepared her admission papers and moved her into the Women's Assessment Unit. Fortunately, Dr Pfizer was at work and came over to meet her soon after she arrived. She spent a few minutes talking to Rosy and then, after a brief examination, called for a scan to be done right away. Rob arrived by then as well. While waiting for the scanner to arrive, Dr Pfizer explained to Rosy and Rob that she agreed with Ms. Wilkinson's assessment that, in fact, Rosy had set into early labor. She did a quick internal assessment and said that the cervix of the uterus was still closed, meaning there was no immediate risk of delivery. She talked to them about what to expect and the next steps to follow. By then, Ms. Wilkinson had arrived as well, and the scanner machine was wheeled in. Dr Pfizer quickly got on with the scanning to make sure that the babies were safe and well. She estimated that Rosy was about 24 weeks pregnant, Twin A weighed approximately 530 grams, and Baby B was nearly 660 grams. Her bag of water around both the twins was intact and adequate. It was obvious that the smaller fetus would be David, as he had not grown well for the last few weeks. While David was in vertex presentation, meaning head down in their mother's womb, his brother Samson was in transverse position across the womb, which meant that it was very likely Rosy may have to undergo a Caesarean section to deliver them. Dr. Pfizer also did some Doppler studies to assess the placental function and opined that David was getting compromised, which meant that the blood flow through his umbilical vessels was showing signs of decrease but not critically at this point for her to worry about any immediate danger to his life. She then told them that she would consider measures to delay the delivery at this stage to get some more time and for them to have a discussion with the Neonatal team. She then prescribed Nifedipine, a drug that is known to relax the uterus, and Betamethasone injections to help mature the babies' lungs. She also instructed her team to inform the neonatal unit about the impending delivery in the next 48 hours or so.

Periviable Consultation

With the increasing survival of extremely premature babies thanks to evidence-based modern newborn care, it has become a practice to counsel families about what to expect when such babies are born. With the survival of the smallest babies comes the burden of increasing stay at the Newborn Intensive Care Unit (NICU) and prolonged stay in the hospital after birth. This puts a lot of burden on the family, especially from an emotional and financial standpoint. There is also the increasing worry about the quality of the survival and the ongoing life-long morbidities that come with it. At 25 weeks of pregnancy, most neonatal centers in the developed world currently give almost 70-80% survival rates but also an adverse neuro developmental morbidity going up to 20 - 40% amongst the survivors. Depending on how you look at it, it is a matter that the parents are to be made aware of, and the neonatal doctors go out of their way to bring these facts to their attention. This is important for the family to know because, after all, at the end of the day, it is the family who will be bearing the brunt. It is now universally accepted amongst neonatal practitioners that babies born after the completion of 24 weeks should be given intensive care, and unless there are gross congenital or genetic abnormalities in the fetus, the family is generally not given the option to limit care, but for babies being born before that period the family can weigh in and make an informed choice of how to proceed. It is, therefore, essential that they are well-informed. Often, however, there may not be enough time for the families to take in all the information, and they opt for continuation of intensive care with the hope that they may take home a healthy baby.

Besides the major concern about brain development, one must realize that being born early is associated with the immaturity of all organ systems, and there may be, at the end of the day, ongoing risks with morbidities related to each organ /system. For example, the lungs, which are immature, get subjected to artificial breathing support to sustain life, which can have negative consequences that may have life-long effects on the survivors. Likewise, every organ that is not yet fully developed could have residual damage from treatment/intervention, and this must be taken into consideration before making a decision.

The intensive care for newborn babies has come a long way. The first premature baby to be offered artificial breathing support happened way back in the early 1960s. Dr Mildred Thorton Stahlman, a Vanderbilt University pediatrician, developed one of the first modern intensive care units for premature babies, helping newborns to breathe with lifesaving new treatments. On Oct. 31, 1961, Dr. Stahlman fitted a premature baby who was gasping for breath into a miniature iron lung machine, also known as a negative pressure ventilator. By the 1970s, negative pressure tanks were jettisoned for positive pressure machines that worked by inflating the lungs. Neonatal Intensive care units have sprung up everywhere in developed countries, and with the ongoing discoveries in the field of perinatal medicine, the number of intact survivors has since increased steadily. Reassuringly, most preterm babies develop into happy, fulfilled children. However, with the increased survival rates of smaller and smaller babies, the number of individuals with morbidities surviving today has increased as well, although the morbidities in proportion are lesser than before. This is putting a burden on the individuals, their families, and the society at large.

Rosy and Robert, being medical trainees themselves, were aware of what was at stake for them. Yet they were keen to meet with the neonatal specialist. An appointment was made for them to meet with the consultant neonatal specialist Dr. Neil. Rosy had known Dr. Neil through her time in rotation in Paediatrics during her 5th-year run. He was an experienced specialist with several years of service in neonatal medicine. She recalled some of the lessons that Dr. Neil had taught during their limited run and had a general impression of his way of looking at his profession. Dr. Neil had varied experience, having worked in different settings around the world before arriving in New Zealand. Rosy knew that he was of Indian origin, having been born and brought up in India. She remembered that he was passionate about teaching and always had the patient and their families' interests at the forefront during his discourses. She, therefore, looked forward to this meeting. Rob had not thought about it, the consequences of this meeting, or what to expect. He had to excuse himself from work that afternoon and felt mildly irked by the prospect. At the appointed time, Dr. Neil presented himself along with a trainee doctor.

Dr. Neil, an experienced neonatologist, was no stranger to the delicate task of counseling parents expecting premature babies. As he prepared to meet Rosy and Robert, first-time parents and doctors themselves, he felt the weight of the moment. He knew that his words would shape their understanding and expectations, influencing their emotions and mindset for the challenging journey ahead.

Years of experience had taught Dr. Neil the importance of balancing honesty with compassion. He understood that delivering factual information about the risks and possible outcomes was crucial, but equally important was providing hope and reassurance. He recalled numerous instances where the right words, spoken with empathy, had made a significant difference in how parents coped with their ordeal.

Before entering the counseling room, Dr. Neil took a moment to gather his thoughts. He reviewed the medical details and considered how best to communicate with them without overwhelming Rosy and Robert. He planned to acknowledge their medical background, recognizing that while they would understand the technicalities, they were also parents about to face an emotional rollercoaster.

Dr. Neil was also prepared to address their questions and concerns with patience, knowing that their professional knowledge might make them more inquisitive and detail-oriented. He reminded himself to be a steady presence, someone they could rely on amidst the uncertainty.

As he stepped into the room, Dr. Neil was ready to offer not just his medical expertise but also his support and empathy. He aimed to provide a clear picture of what to expect while also fostering a sense of hope and resilience. For Dr. Neil, this was not just about delivering information—it was about connecting with

Rosy and Robert on a human level, guiding them through one of the most challenging times of their lives.

After the usual introductions, he laid out what was in store for them. He went about checking how much they knew exactly and slowly updated them about the process of how the impending delivery would be managed by the newborn unit team. They were made aware of what to expect when a decision is made by the obstetric team to deliver the twins. They were also given a run down on the various issues that they need to be aware of, specifically with the birth of their twin babies at 25 weeks. They knew that it was going to be tough on them. They could expect to be in the unit for at least several weeks, if not months, depending on how things went. There would always be support for their own well-being with a team consisting of social workers and other professionals to take care of their needs on standby. Dr. Neil concluded by asking them to clarify any issues that they may have with a promise to answer all their queries to the best of his knowledge and experience in dealing with their specific situation. Rosy and Rob wanted to know about the chances of survival for David and the specific consequences of the early birth that would be brought upon Samson because of David's condition. They also wondered about what if they decided against the proposal to deliver them early. They had been talked to at length by the obstetrician and the midwifery team, but they wanted to know what Dr. Neil thought about it. Dr. Neil said that it is a decision for the obstetricians to take and the family to make, but he, being aware of what was discussed, opined that delivering the twins was in the best interest of both the twins. This gave them a chance for David to survive, which was very unlikely if he were to continue in the womb; if he perished in the womb, that would have adverse consequences to Samson's life and, importantly, his brain development in the womb. He then advised them to go with what they thought was best now that they were fully informed. The Neonatal and Obstetrics team would support any decision that they take. He promised to come back again after they had time to deliberate on what was discussed, and he also invited them to have a tour of the NewBorn Intensive Care Unit (NICU) to get a feel of the place and interact with the nursing and other support staff to help make up their mind.

Rosy and Robert had no doubt about what they wished. They did want everything done to save both their twins. They were willing to accept the statistics on mortality and morbidity. Rosy was optimistic and positive that the better part of the probability would prevail, and Rob, the realist, was happy for whichever way it went. They decided to go for the NICU tour, not realizing how different it looked from the patient's perspective. The divide between them as doctors and now as would-be parents was wide and came as a rude realization. They met with the nursing staff, other support staff, and some parents. When they left the tour, they were not sure if it was a good idea. The interaction with the nursing staff was lovely; they found them to be very friendly and welcoming, but they were a bit disgruntled when meeting with some of the parents. They were a mix: some very happy, some indifferent, but a few were teary and frightened. Obviously, each parent had a unique situation to deal with, and Rosy felt a bit depressed. Rob, realizing how Rosy was feeling, tried to change the topic of conversation and put up a brave front. It was already getting late; they went to the antenatal ward, where a bed was prepared for Rosy to stay in for the next few days, and Rob left after a few minutes.

Newborn Intensive Care Unit

The Newborn Intensive Care Unit (NICU) is often a place of intense emotions, where hope and fear coexist. Parents of premature or critically ill newborns navigate a rollercoaster of emotions, facing medical challenges that can be overwhelming. Yet, amidst the harrowing moments, there are also glimmers of light—small, precious moments that provide solace and joy. These lighter moments offer a necessary balance to the otherwise tough period in the NICU, reminding parents of the resilience of their tiny fighters and the strength of their own love.

One of the most profound moments for parents in the NICU is the first time they get to touch their baby. Despite the incubators and wires, this simple act of connection can be incredibly uplifting. The warmth of a tiny hand gripping a parent's finger brings a flood of emotions, reinforcing the bond that transcends the clinical environment.

Every little milestone in the NICU is a cause for celebration. Whether it's the first time the baby opens their eyes, their first successful feeding, or the first time they breathe without assistance, these moments are victories. Parents often document these milestones with photos and journals, creating cherished memories of their baby's journey.

Humor becomes a coping mechanism in the NICU. Parents and staff alike find comfort in light-hearted moments. A baby's unexpected smile, a funny noise, or a playful gesture can bring laughter and relief. Nurses often share jokes or light stories to keep spirits high, creating a sense of camaraderie and support.

Kangaroo care, where parents hold their baby skin-to-skin, is both a medical practice and an emotional balm. These sessions provide warmth and comfort to the baby while giving parents a sense of purpose and closeness. The joy of feeling their baby's heartbeat and the rise and fall of their tiny chest can be an immensely grounding experience.

Decorating the baby's area with photos, drawings, and little mementos can transform the sterile environment of the NICU into a more comforting space. Parents often bring in favorite toys, blankets, or family pictures, adding a personal touch that makes the NICU feel a bit more like home.

Parents in the NICU often form close bonds with other families who are going through similar experiences. They celebrate each other's milestones, share advice, and offer emotional support. These relationships can be a source of strength and joy, fostering a sense of community and shared resilience.

The NICU staff plays a crucial role in providing care and support. Their compassionate gestures, comforting words, and tireless efforts create a positive atmosphere. Parents often form deep connections with the nurses, seeing them not just as caregivers but as allies in their journey.

The Delivery

The next couple of days went by quickly. The team in the Newborn unit was informed by their Obstetric counterparts about their decision to go ahead with the delivery. Following that, time was spent preparing Rosy for delivery in the next 48 hours. She was given the medications Nifedipine to delay delivery temporarily and Betamethasone to get the lungs of her twins to mature rapidly.

Rosy's time was consumed thinking about what Dr. Neil had mentioned during the counseling session. She had resisted going to google to check out what is going on in the field of research in the care of premature babies but eventually gave in and was quite intrigued to learn that the field of neonatal medicine is still relatively in its infancy. The modern version of care for premature babies was kick-started by a political event. It was the birth of the son of the president of America, Robert Kennedy, in the early 1960s. The baby was named Patrick Bouvier Kennedy. Patrick was born prematurely, and despite all efforts from the top doctors of that time, he sadly passed away. He died due to immaturity of his lungs. At that time, there was no method available to sustain the life of babies with immature lungs. Following this, the Government of the USA allocated a lot of funding & resources for research, which has, over the last few decades, resulted in many innovations and discoveries that have changed the outcome for prematurely born babies dramatically. One of the first developments was the use of artificial breathing support for these babies. One other important development in the field came from

New Zealand, where the legendary perinatal physician Sir Graham Collingwood (Mont) Liggin, on whose name exists the famous Liggins Institute in Auckland, and his colleagues discovered that by giving the medicine betamethasone (a Steroid) to pregnant women threatening to deliver prematurely, the lung maturity of these babies can be hastened. The research work coming from this institute has gone a long way in improving the outcome of premature babies the world over. Another drug that is currently administered to women expecting very premature babies is magnesium sulfate, which, when given to women within about four hours of delivery, has shown benefit in improving the neurodevelopmental outcome, specifically the issue of cerebral palsy (CP). Prematurity is one of the well-recognized causes of CP. It used to occur with a frequency of one in two hundred births worldwide. This statistic remained robustly unchanged for nearly a hundred years since its first description by an English physician, William John Little, in the late 1880s, hence also called Little's disease. Thanks to the relentless work from doctors and scientists all over the world in the field of perinatal medicine, we are beginning to see a change for the better, with a proportionately lesser number of extremely premature babies developing CP in the last couple of decades. However, with the increasing number of extremely premature babies now surviving, one could expect to see this statistic offset by more absolute numbers of CP victims in the community. CP is not the only problem that survivors of extreme premature birth must deal with in the long term. As mentioned before, every organ system is at risk of developing residual damage from the effects of intensive care over and above the unnatural process of protecting, developing, and maturing life for these babies outside the natural environment of the womb.

Rosy was jolted from the reverie by the obstetric consultant. She was rounding with her team of registrars and nursing staff. She informed Rosy that she would be first on the list for the cesarean section the next day. There would be a formal consenting process to go through along with some pre-op blood work up that day. If all goes well as planned, Rosy will need to go nil by mouth by about 4 am for her to be ready for anesthesia at 10 am. There was a choice of spinal (epidural) anesthesia as opposed to general anesthesia. The difference is that in spinal anesthesia, one is given anesthetic drugs through the spinal vertebral space, and that anesthetizes at a certain level below the chosen vertebra. The individual remains awake but pain-free compared to general anesthesia, where you are knocked out completely. Rosy was to undergo spinal as the chosen modality. She knew from her training that the complications to herself and the babies are generally lower with spinal anesthesia. Besides, she was keen to be part of any decision-making that would be needed at delivery.

Rosy and Rob had already consented to both twins receiving vitamin K injections. This is the standard practice to protect against what is called the "Haemorrhagic disease of the Newborn," a dreaded disease now almost eliminated. As the name suggests, newborn babies with this condition tend to bleed from the cut umbilical stump and, at times, bleed spontaneously inside the vital organs, like the brain, within a few days of birth. This can result in serious catastrophic events like brain damage or even death if the baby does not get an emergency blood transfusion. Vitamin K is essential for the production of proteins, otherwise called coagulation factors in the liver. For reasons not well understood, unlike most vitamins, the babies do not get enough vitamin K through the placenta, nor is there enough of this in the mother's milk. Being born very premature only aggravates the situation many fold. It is important to mention here that, of late, there is a tendency for some families to refuse this vital preventive measure based on a misconception that Vit K given at birth can increase the risk of childhood cancers like leukaemia. This came about from a faulty study published in the early nineties by the scientist Dr J Golding and others from the Institute of Child Health, Royal Hospital for Sick Children, Bristol. Despite multiple subsequent studies clearly demystifying this belief, a small but sadly growing number of people believe in this myth and put their babies at risk. These are the same people, most times, who do not believe in vaccinating their children against many yesteryear killer diseases like polio, measles, chicken pox, tetanus, whooping cough, etc. As a result, the world is sadly seeing a re-emergence of these diseases, some of which were once considered to be eliminated.

The next day, at the appointed time, the Neonatal team, headed by Dr. Neil, was in the operation theatre as Rosy was wheeled in along with Rob, who accompanied her. As the Anaesthetic team was preparing to give the epidural, the neonatal team prepared two sets of resuscitation stations ready to receive the twins. The nurse in charge of the theatre did the usual round of identifying every individual in the theatre and checking everyone's role. Once the go-ahead was obtained from the anesthetist, the obstetric team went ahead with the operation, in Rosy's case, in the lower segment of the cesarean section. Twin A (David) was delivered first and handed over to the neonatal team after the customary one-minute wait (called delayed cord clamping) before clamping the cord, followed a few minutes later by the birth of Samson. Both twins were generally vigorous at birth, and they made some attempts at crying soon after they were lifted out from the womb. Both, however, needed breathing support in the form of continuous positive airway pressure (CPAP) soon after they were placed in their respective resuscitation trays. Once they were stabilized, Rob was invited to cut their umbilical cords. The vitamin K was given intramuscularly and readied for transfer to the newborn unit for further care. As they were wheeled out of the theatre, they were brought close to the operation table so Rosy could see them from close and touch them. Rosy closed her eyes briefly as she touched them each and prayed silently. Apgar Scores were allocated to both by their respective team. David was judged to have a score of 7 and 8 for Samson, both having done reasonably well.

Apgar Scoring, as an important objective measure of the condition of babies at birth, was introduced by the legendary Dr. Virginia Apgar, who was a pioneering American anesthesiologist. She developed the Score named after her in 1952. This simple yet revolutionary scoring system assesses the health of newborns immediately after birth, focusing on five criteria, remembered by medical students as a mnemonic after her name: **A**ppearance(color), **P**ulse(heart rate), **G**rimace(reflex response to handling), <u>A</u>ctivity(muscle tone), and <u>R</u>espiration(rate of breathing). The score is given at one and five minutes post-delivery to quickly determine if a newborn needs urgent additional medical care. A best score of 2 is given to each criterion; thus, the maximum score one could get is 10/10. Apgar's innovation significantly reduced infant mortality rates and laid the foundation for modern neonatology. The Apgar score was developed largely for babies born at full-term gestation. It has limitations when used alone for extremely premature babies. Premature infants often have lower scores due to their underdeveloped physiology, which might not accurately reflect their overall health or the immediate need for medical intervention. Neonatologists typically use additional assessments and monitoring tailored to the specific needs of premature infants to ensure they receive appropriate care. It's important to consider the Apgar score as one part of a comprehensive evaluation rather than a standalone measure for these vulnerable newborns.

The decision to weigh them was deferred till they reached the newborn unit. Rob briefly kissed Rosy on her forehead, bid goodbye, and accompanied the teams to the newborn unit while the obstetric and the anesthetic team continued to work on Rosy.

Early Newborn Care

The newborn unit team was ready to receive the twins. There is a team of medical and nursing personnel on standby whenever a planned admission is expected. The cots are prewarmed, and the necessary equipment for care and monitors are kept ready for use. The babies are usually weighed before being moved into the cots. Birthweight is a very important anthropometric measure that would determine how much fluids, calories, proteins, fats, and other nutrients the babies would require. It also forms the basis for the calculation of the dose of medications needed. Birthweight also determines if a preterm baby is adequately grown in the womb. Babies are generally categorized into three groups based on their weight and gestation: adequately grown or appropriate for gestation (AGA), small for gestation (SGA), and large for gestation (LGA), respectively. This classification sets up the immediate care plans. SGA and LGA babies are at higher risk for immediate and long-term problems over and above those due to their level of prematurity compared to AGA babies at every gestation. The immediate care and monitoring priorities fall into the following domains: Support of breathing and blood circulation, Temperature maintenance, Prevention of infection, Nutritional support, and support for the family's well-being. To achieve this, premature babies are hooked on appropriate respiratory support devices based on their breathing effort. Generally, very premature and extremely premature babies are placed into incubators for temperature support, and depending on the risks for infection, most babies currently get started on some sort of prophylactic (preventive) antibiotic cover. Family support often gets relegated to the last, but it remains one of the cornerstones for care in the newborn unit, and current research is emphasizing the need for parental involvement in care from the very beginning for optimal outcomes. While the nursing and medical team attend to the admission process, the family is talked to by the most senior physician on the floor and is assisted by an inhouse social worker in most setups.

Rob, who had accompanied the team to the newborn unit, was familiar with the process, having spent some time in the unit during his medical school run. Dr. Neil updated him nevertheless about what was going on and encouraged him to seek clarification on any issues that he may have. He was also informed that Rosy and he would have unlimited 24-hour access as parents and was introduced to the social worker, Ms. Lorraine, who would advise them about the support services available, including the professional services for emotional and psychological needs for parents, which will form an important part of long- term care.

David, who was the first twin to be delivered, weighed 510 grams, while the second twin, Samson, weighed 620 grams. While these weights would be considered appropriate for their GA, clearly, David was beginning to show the effects of placental insufficiency and, hence, the discrepancy in their weights. David was beginning to receive lower blood supply, hence the weight discrepancy.

The admission process involved inserting catheters(plastic tubes) into the umbilical veins and arteries, followed by checking their positions by X-ray to make sure that their tips are not lying adjacent to the various branches supplying or draining blood that can impede this function. This is a tricky encounter and needs skills. It is important that this is done efficiently and quickly. Current recommendations are that this be done as close to within the first hour of the birthing process called the "Golden Hour." It is important that this is done while keeping in mind the guiding principle of minimal handling, cardiorespiratory, and temperature stability during the process. It is not always possible to get this right, even when attempted by expert hands, but in the case of David and Samson, they were lucky that it all went smoothly and successfully. The next step would involve collecting and sending blood samples to check for the oxygen level, acid-base, electrolyte, and potential infection risk parameters. Soon after that, the venous and arterial lines are secured, and fluid is connected to maintain hydration, nutrition, and vital sign monitoring.

Premature babies, and for that matter, even term-born babies, have excess fluid in their bodies at birth. There is a natural process in which this excess fluid is eliminated mainly through the kidneys as urine; some losses can occur through the skin and from the breath. However, unlike in term-born babies, in a premature baby, the kidneys are not mature enough to do this function efficiently, and the skin being thinner and of a larger surface area compared to their weight, they lose much more than desirable rapidly, leading to dehydration and its consequences. At the same time, they have the immaturity of the gastrointestinal system that prevents adequate amounts of fluid and nutrition from being given by mouth, hence the need for fluid by intravenous route. As mentioned before, in addition to the immaturity of the kidneys and gastrointestinal system, every other system like the nervous, cardiorespiratory, immune, and metabolic functions are immature, leading to a risk for bleeding in the brain, lower blood pressure, increasing oxygen requirement due to inadequacy of their lungs to exchange blood gases, low blood sugar, and infection from setting in. The initial blood tests and X-rays done at admission help guide the treating team in checking for most of these and making the necessary corrections and/or instituting appropriate treatment as necessary. At this stage, the only factor that cannot be assessed adequately is if any bleeding has already occurred in the brain. For that, the doctors use bedside ultrasound devices but not necessarily immediately unless there is a clear indication that bleeding may have occurred, like a drop in blood pressure or low levels of hemoglobin.

Fortunately for the twins, this process also went smoothly without any adverse effects on any system except that David's blood sugar level came as low (less than 2.6 millimoles/Litre), for which he was given extra glucose in his intravenous line. However, as the hours passed by, both the twins started showing the need for increasing oxygen requirement, and they started working harder to breathe, indicating that both are developing a common problem called "respiratory distress syndrome (RDS)," also known as "Hyaline membrane disease (HMD)" because of a membrane-like structure lining the inner surface of the alveoli were observed by pathologists on autopsy specimens collected in babies who died of RDS in the early years of this special branch of medicine.

Respiratory Distress Syndrome (RDS)

RDS or HMD is a problem that premature babies uniquely suffer from because of the deficiency of a naturally occurring chemical substance in the lungs called surfactant. Over 50% of babies who are born extremely premature (at < 28 weeks) develop RDS.

In the late 1950s, Dr Mary Allen Avery and colleagues from Harvard School of Public Health identified the cause for this syndrome as a deficiency of surfactant. Surfactant is a chemical substance produced by the inner lining cells of the air sacs (alveoli). It helps keep the alveoli open even when the air containing more carbon dioxide is exhaled during the exhalation phase of breathing. Lack of surfactant causes collapse of the alveolar sacs and the lungs, which makes breathing for the baby harder and harder against a partially closed glottis (the opening into the windpipe- trachea), thus generating a back pressure to keep their alveoli open but over time they get tired and give in, leading to what is known as respiratory failure.

It is only in the last few decades that surfactant became available as a medication to be instilled into the lungs through the trachea. This has vastly helped save premature babies in recent times. The twins both needed administration of the surfactant, which required them to be intubated, meaning inserting a plastic tube (endotracheal tube) into the trachea and following this, they were connected to ventilators (artificial breathing machines).

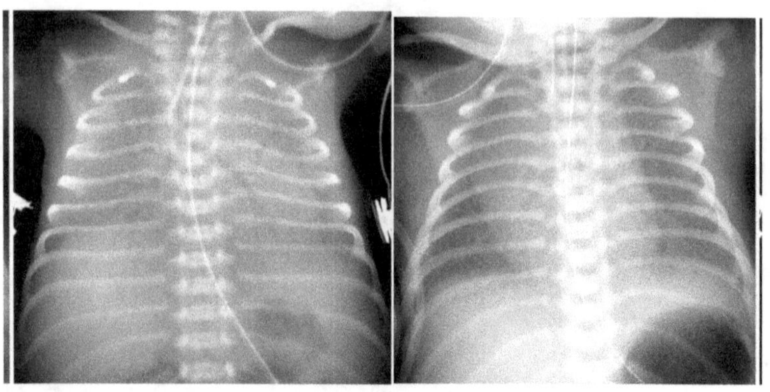

Chest X-Ray: HMD Dense Lungs & Expanded lungs after surfactant instillation

Of late, this process has become less invasive with the use of less invasive methods called the LISA (Less Invasive Surfactant Administration), where the instillation is done with tubes that are not retained and babies not put on the breathing machine. Every time the lung collapses, it requires more pressure to open it, and with it comes injuries that result in what is called inflammation. The four cardinal signs of inflammation - swelling *(tumor)*, pain *(dolor)*, increase in local temperature *(calor)*, and redness *(rubor)*, like what one would experience when one gets injured externally were described by Aulus Cornelius Celsus (25 BC-50 AD), a Roman encyclopedist. This is the body's defense mechanism, but when the healing occurs later, it is often accompanied by scar formation, like in external injuries, which leads to difficulty breathing and chronic dependence on extra oxygen and breathing supports. More about this later.

David needed less intervention because his degree of respiratory distress and oxygen requirement were lesser than

Samson's. This is not unusual because the former suffered a degree of stress in the womb. During stress, the body produces a hormone called steroid to cope with stressful situations and induces the production of surfactant. Samson, being less stressed, had the disadvantage of not having enough surfactant. This is the rationale for the use of steroids antenatally in threatened preterm birth. All over the world, the practice of antenatal steroids has become standard since a number of randomized controlled clinical trials have confirmed the benefit. Even so, the benefit is only about 50% effective in the sense that it helps, but it may not entirely rule out the need for surfactant administration.

Once they are on the artificial breathing support, the next step the doctors aim for is a period of stability followed by a decrease in the need for oxygen. Although surfactant allows for a gradual decrease in oxygen, in most cases for air, sometimes the effect is not sustained, needing the use of another dose within the next 6 to 12 hours. While David continued to remain in the air, Sam needed another dose before his need for respiratory support could be reduced, delaying the process of his extubation (removal of the breathing tube). Thus, he suffered the consequence of premature birth more than David at this stage. The longer the tube is left in, the greater and prolonged the inflammatory response and the greater the chance of chronic dependence on oxygen. David was extubated the next day and put on continuous positive airway pressure (CPAP) via nasal prongs.

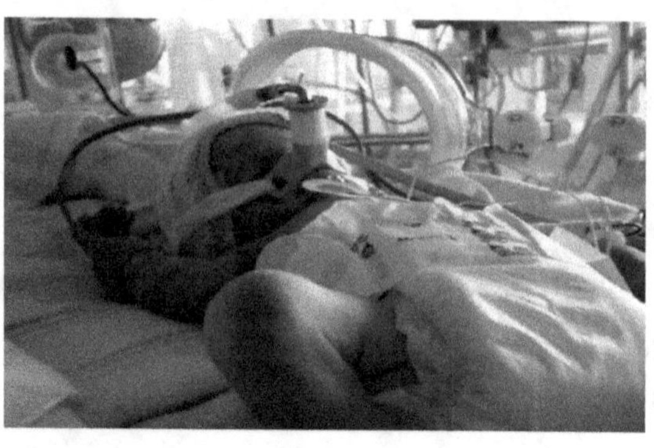

(Picture of a baby on Nasal CPAP)

CPAP is a therapeutic modality for countering RDS in premature babies that came into existence in the early 70s following the research work of Dr. George A Gregory and others from the department of Anaesthesia, University of California, who worked on the premise that by continuing to give back pressure one can keep the alveoli from collapsing. Despite the availability of surfactant, this remains the cornerstone of respiratory support to date. Samson developed another complication from the respiratory support called pulmonary interstitial emphysema (PIE), meaning extravasation of air from the air sacs(alveoli) into the tissue outside supporting the alveolar structure carrying the blood vessels, which deliver carbon dioxide produced in the various cells within the body as a part of the process of blood circulation and Oxygen from the breathed from the air to the body. The process of blood circulation through veins and arteries takes oxygen to be distributed to the cells of the body for metabolism and take away carbon dioxide to the lungs for exhalation, ensuring gas exchange. When one develops PIE, the alveoli get compressed (collapse), perpetuating the need for prolonged and increased respiratory support and difficulty with gas exchange, with all its short- and long-term consequences. Short-term complications being the propensity to infection (ventilator-associated pneumonia) because of the invasive nature of breathing support through a foreign body in the form of a breathing tube (endotracheal tube). We will discuss long-term complications later. Samson needed careful adjustment to his settings on the breathing machine before he could be extubated on the seventh day of his life. The whole process of respiratory support involves a lot of handling, pain, and destabilization, causing fluctuation in the blood supply of the brain, which increases the risk of bleeding, also called Intraventricular Hemorrhage (IVH). The earlier the destabilization is in life, the higher the risk of bleeding and the severity. There are other reasons for bleeding in the brain in premature babies, which is one of the dreaded complications that we will see in the next chapter.

IntraVentricular Haemorrhage (IVH)

Both twins had their head ultrasound examination done on the fifth day of their life, as per protocol in the NICU. While Samson escaped any bleed, David had what is called a grade 3 IVH bilaterally, meaning bleeding into the lateral ventricular space (cavities) of his brain on both sides. In addition to the lateral ventricles, the brain has cavities extending down into the spinal cord called the third and fourth ventricles, as shown in the picture below.

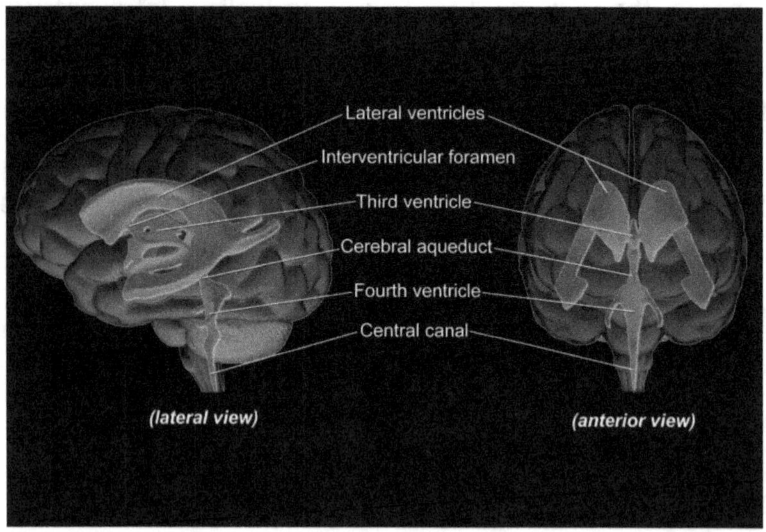

This came as devastating news for his parents, to his mother Rosy in particular. She was dreading this thought because of the complications that it would entail. Dr. Neil, the neonatologist who performed this test, invited the parents to be by the bedside when he planned to do the test. Rosy was apprehensive. She had read up on IVH and was dreading the thought. Only Rosy could attend as Rob was busy with his work in the cardiology department. Dr. Neil explained to Rosy what he was looking for and why it was important.

Around 10- 15% of babies born very premature, like the Tam twins, tend to bleed in the brain. This is believed to be because of various factors, such as the immature brain not having enough support for the delicate and fragile blood vessel network called capillaries, making it easy to rupture from changes in blood pressure. However, in the more mature babies and beyond, the changes in the systemic blood pressure do not affect the blood pressure within the blood vessels in the brain (cerebral BP) due to a mechanism called autoregulation, which is not well developed in premature babies. The systemic blood pressure itself is not well regulated in tiny preterm babies. It fluctuates widely and can raise abruptly in the baby during crying or handling during care, hence the importance of minimal handling as a dictum of care for these babies. Most bleeds, however, are generally small, meaning the bleed is unlikely to cause any serious consequences in the short and long term. Grade I (minor bleeding) are usually small in volume and confined to the inner lining of the ventricles. In grades II, the blood spills into the ventricle (cavities within the brain, which are normally filled with a fluid called cerebrospinal fluid) but is small enough not to cause an increase in the size of the ventricles. On the other hand, major bleeds, grade III and IV, are seen in 3-5% of extreme preterm babies. In grade III bleed, the amount of blood is large enough to cause distension of the ventricles but is still confined to the ventricles, unlike in grade IV, where the bleed is often in the periventricular region of the brain, hence called periventricular hemorrhage (PVH), meaning bleeding into the substance of the brain surrounding the ventricles, in addition to bleeding of different volumes within the ventricles as well. The grade IV bleed is believed to be a venous infarct, wherein there is clotting of the venous channels draining blood from that region of the brain with the associated bleeding both into the ventricle and the surrounding brain matter. Both the grades of major bleeds III and IV have the potential for significant complications immediately and in the long-term.

Grades of intraventricular hemorrhage
(cross-section view of the brain)

Grade I: bleeding near ventricle

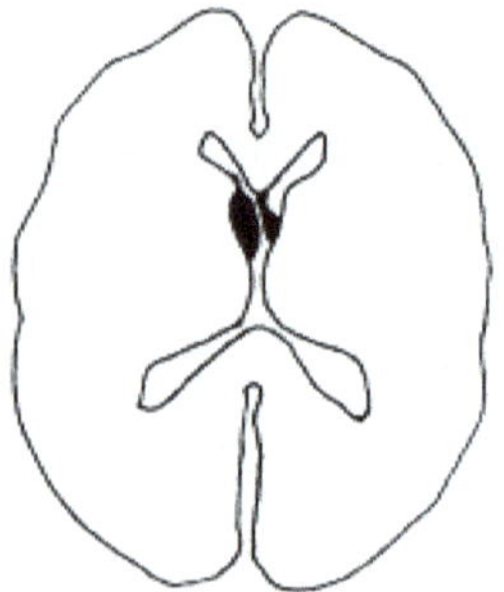

Grade II: Blood in ventricle

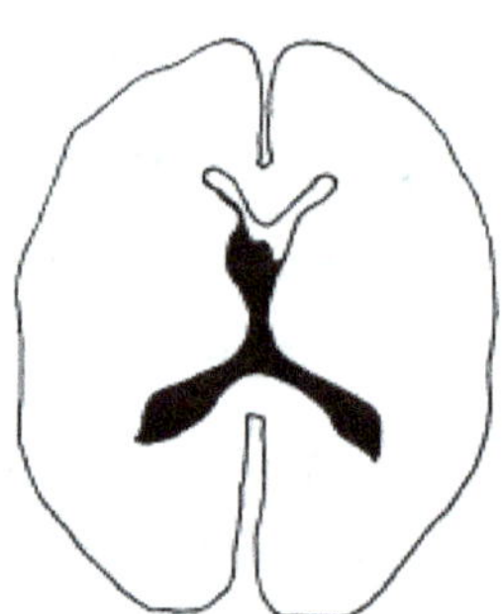

Grade III: Enlarged ventricle

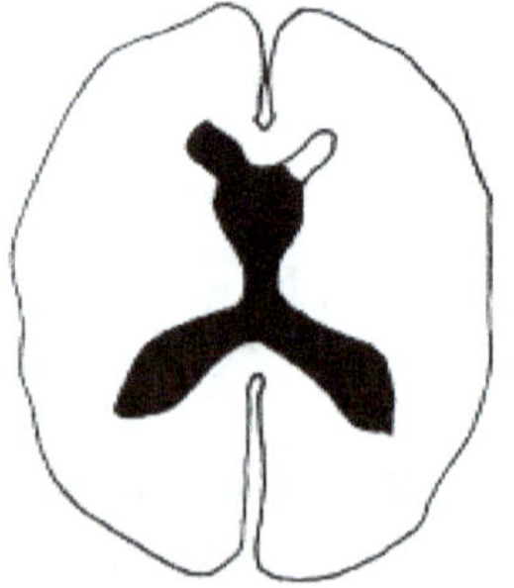

Grade IV: Enlarged ventricle with blood in brain tissue

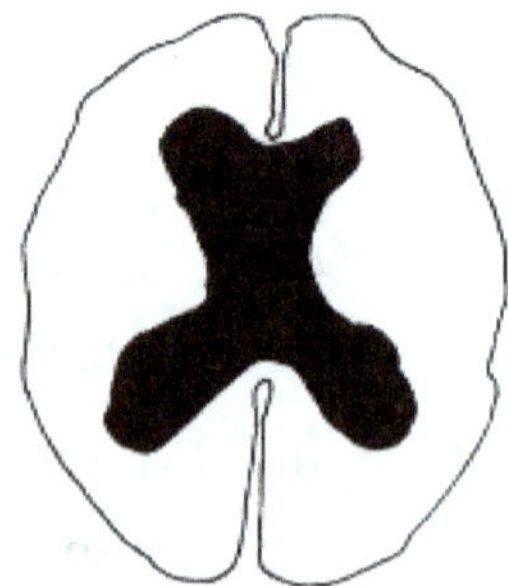

Blood in the ventricles can obstruct the flow of the cerebrospinal fluid (CSF) from the lateral ventricles to the third and fourth ventricles and beyond, resulting in what is called hydrocephalus or simply fluid accumulation in the ventricular spaces that causes the ventricles to balloon out. Very often, this will eventually resolve spontaneously, but in a small but significant proportion of babies, it would continue to increase the size of the ventricles and, with it, the size of the head. This has the potential to impact brain growth. So, to prevent this, one may need to take measures to contain the increase by tapping the ventricles intermittently and/or by inserting a shunt from the ventricles to the peritoneal cavity in the abdomen (ventriculo-peritoneal (VP) shunt) that then becomes a source for further complication in the form of infection, blockage and need for replacement, all involving further surgeries. The grade IV bleeds, in addition, have the potential to damage the nerve tracts traversing through the affected areas of the brain, especially the long tracts that carry the nerve endings going down from the brain surface to the limbs. Depending upon how severe the bleeding is and whether it is one-sided or both sides, it could result in significant immediate complications, as severe as deaths, to long-term problems of neuro-developmental delays and cerebral palsy.

David's grade III bleed would need close monitoring by way of measuring his head size more frequently than usual, as well as repeated head ultrasound examinations. Rosy was aware of the consequences and was worried enough to become anxious. She started becoming depressed and stressed, leading to disturbed sleep. This also affected her milk supply, which she was already struggling to keep going. She was referred to the lactation consultant and to the "True Colour" services, which deals with emotional support. True Colour is an external organization run by a group of very talented and dedicated professionals with backgrounds in nursing, psychology, and social service. They have done yeoman service over the years and were recently recognized by the government at the national day commemoration. It is not uncommon for parents of preterm babies who struggle to cope to go into depression, affecting the overall care of their babies. One of the well-recognized premises of care is the involvement of parents in the care, as mentioned before. This may involve handling, cuddling, and assisting the nursing staff. It has been shown to improve the overall outcome and is now universally encouraged and practiced worldwide. In a recent communique, the WHO described the practice of "Kangaroo Care" as an essential part of the care of newborn babies born prematurely in the developing and underdeveloped world where the resources are limited because of the overwhelming evidence of the benefit for survival in such settings. Kangaroo care, a mode of care that originated in South America in the later part of the last century, involves the babies being held by the parents on their chest for varying periods every day as allowed by their clinical stability.

Rob was also quite disappointed and frustrated with this turn of events. He became increasingly irritable, and it started showing at work as well. He decided to take a break and spend more time with Rosy and their twins. The role that dads play in the outcome of their premature babies is only being recognized recently. He sought an appointment with Dr. Neil, who had not seen him for a while. Dr. Neil was more than happy to sit with Robert and explain what was going on. The frustration often felt by dads is because of being not included/ignored or not being able to make it to such meetings with their baby's caregivers as often as they could. Another big frustrating factor is the fear of the unknown. Most of the time, in medicine, one can only make an informed guess based on previous experience and data from the literature. Rob, being a doctor, understood this very well and kept worrying about the worst possibilities. He was also aware of the risk of attaching probabilities from population-based studies to individual circumstances. Every individual is unique, and the only way one can be certain is by considering the individual's unique characteristics for prediction. The practice of medicine has not yet reached that state of sophistication of what is called precision medicine. All these weighed heavily on Rob's mind. However, he realized that a heart-to-heart talk with Dr. Neil would still be a good move to help him move forward.

The next afternoon, a meeting was booked with the parents. Rosy's and Rob's parents were keen to join, but they decided not to bring them along. The discussion went along the expected lines, with Dr. Neil introducing his team of nursing staff and Ms. Lorraine, the social worker. He elicited from the distraught parents their understanding of where they are with the status of their infants and if they had any complaints or clarification about the care. Rosy was very sad and with her downcast eyes, she just nodded to indicate that she had nothing to complain about or clarify. Rob, on the other hand, wanted to know whether anything could be done to salvage David's IVH. Dr. Neil responded by outlining the plan of care by way of closer monitoring and reassured that the chances of further extension of the bleed were minimal. However, there was still the risk of short-term complications like hydrocephalus (enlargement of the cavities in the brain with excess fluid), and he told them again that it was rare in most cases, but only time would tell. He realized that Rob was more interested in its long-term implications and the neurodevelopmental delay that he was dreading. Dr. Neil said that the long-term outcome depends on several factors and that they must be realistic about some degree of risk with developmental delay over and above the basic risk rate for the twins from just being born so prematurely. It was hardly any relief to Rob, but he appreciated the honesty in Dr. Neil's remarks. Realizing what Rob was thinking, the doctor explained how one should remain positive and hope for the best. There are good rehabilitative measures available that would reduce the impact of the damage by early and effective interventions. Besides, he said that the data shows that the better outcome also depends on many other factors: the loving and caring atmosphere at home and the investment parents are willing to put in for a favorable outcome. He concluded by pointing out the fact that with both of them being concerned intellectuals, one can naturally expect David to be not far from his peers in intellectual development. Dr. Neil also impressed on them that it is too early in the course to start worrying about long-term consequences but reassured them that with the first week behind them, they can look forward to better times and how important it is for them to remain positive and be involved in the care of their children. With that, the meeting concluded, and he left the social worker, Ms. Lorraine, to spend more time with them. Ms. Lorraine outlined all the avenues available to support them through the situation and in the future. She insisted that getting their parents to come in may not be a bad idea. Rosy was already in touch with the True Colours. In times like this family support plays a huge role.

Till now, the grandparents were not aware of the bleeding, and both Mary and Rob had refrained their parents from coming over, mainly because they did not want them to start worrying. After the meeting, they had second thoughts, mainly because Rob was also getting worried about Rosy's fragile mental state. He realized that Rosy might benefit from her parent's support but was wary of his own parents coming over. Rosy reluctantly agreed to let only her parents be involved at that stage.

Rosy's parents, who had already relocated to Hamilton, were more than happy to be involved. They were feeling sad for Rosy, not knowing what was causing so much stress. They could not bear to see their only child suffering and were willing to do anything to help her recover. When they were eventually told about David's brain bleed, they were more relieved than saddened to know why Rosy had suddenly become so depressed. They decided to take her home and nurse her back to health. Meanwhile, Rob insisted that he wanted his parents not to be informed, and Rosy had no energy or inclination to fight.

So, Rosy finally went home to her parent's place in Hamilton. The next day, they met up with Ms Wilkinson, Rosy's midwife.

Rosy's parents requested a house visit, and during their meeting, they decided that it would be better to seek mental health advice for Rosy, to which Rosy and Rob agreed. Rosy was seen by the Mental health nurse the next day and commenced on antidepressants. Rosy was worried that it might interfere with her breast milk supply, but after a consultation with Dr. Neil and the lactation consultant, Ms. Raewyn, her fear of the medication being excreted in breast milk was addressed. Some medications used for maternal mental health issues are excreted in sufficient amounts in the mother's milk, which can have effects on the baby's health, but recent studies in this area have identified drugs that are either not excreted in the breast milk at all or excreted in minimal amounts to have any effect on their babies. A routine was set up for Rosy to express her breast milk and for it to be delivered to the NICU. Rob spent much of his break from work to attend to the babies' needs, carrying the expressed breast milk and providing Kangaroo care to the babies. In time, the situation improved, and Rosy recovered enough to start attending to the babies by the time Rob's break came to an end.

Watchful Expectancy and
Masterly Inactivity

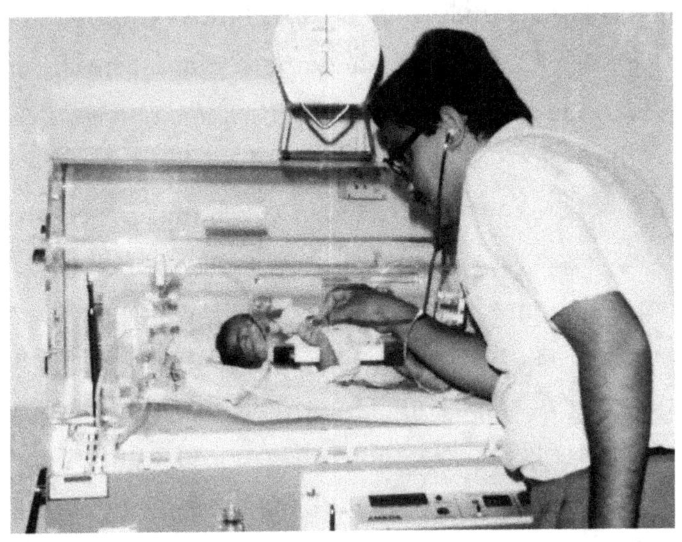

The next few weeks were spent observing and monitoring the various medical aspects of the babies. David's head size was monitored with an ultrasound of the head twice weekly. There was a tendency for his head size to grow faster than Sam's with an increase in the volume of the ventricles, but thankfully, it remained below the threshold for intervention. A large majority of bleeds tend to resolve with a minor increase in the size of the ventricles, and this phenomenon is called arrested hydrocephalus.

While Sam was growing satisfactorily, David started showing poor growth. Rosy was able to sustain adequate milk output, but her breast milk alone was not sufficient. One of the ways to tackle this was by adding extra calories, proteins, vitamins, and minerals in the form of what is called the Human Milk Fortifiers (HMF).

These products are now available in the market and often resourced by newborn units all over the world. These are produced from cow milk and come with their own issues. There are companies in the USA and others manufacturing it from donated human milk, but it is not yet available in New Zealand. Besides, these are very expensive, and recent data reveals that they may not be much better than cow's milk-based products. Most babies tolerate HMF well, but some would find certain products that do not agree with their gut, causing bloating and intolerance. In a small proportion, it can cause milk protein allergy in babies whose family members may be susceptible to this problem. Dr. Neil discussed this with Rosy and Rob and, with their expressed consent, commenced it for the twins. There was no history of allergy to milk proteins on either side of the parents and their families. However, within a day of starting HMF, both twins started showing signs of intolerance in the form of abdominal distension and general unsettledness. There are differing opinions amongst the specialists about this being a cause, but generally, they agree to continue with it as long as it is a minor problem.

However, there is a dreaded condition called Necrotising Enterocolitis (NEC) that Neonatal specialists are always worried about. This can afflict the preterm babies around two to three weeks of age as the milk volume input increases. It is a devastating disease that can cause damage to the delicate intestines of these babies and, in the worst cases, would cause emergency abdominal surgery or even death. The cause for this is not well understood yet, but the immaturity of the gut from being born premature plays a big role. Lately, there has been research showing that the bacteria that normally colonize the gut of every one of us differs from those in babies in the NICU. There are friendly bacteria that every one of us acquires at birth, but in the NICU environment, these are altered, allowing harmful bacteria to set in and outgrow. So, as a rule, in most of the units in Australasia and the rest of the world, premature babies are started on probiotics- bacteria that are beneficial with the hope that they will outgrow the harmful bacteria. Both twins had already started on the probiotics as soon as they were born. Research from this part of the world has shown that this practice reduces the incidence of NEC. Dr. Neil warned the parents about NEC, and Rosy started worrying again. She requested if the HMF could be stopped or withheld for a few days. However, the medical team convinced her that growth is an important part of the babies' neurodevelopment and general health. This is the delicate path that the medical team and the parents must tread in their long journey in the NICU. Every intervention has the potential to cause harm, and the decision-making is a delicate balance between benefit and harm.

In addition to the management problem, there was still the need for non-invasive respiratory support. This by itself causes distension of the abdomen, as gas, a mixture of air and oxygen, is pumped under certain pressure when using nasal CPAP support. Part of it gets into the gut. Most units would have protocols to tackle this issue, but the fact remains that it can interfere with feeding and general well-being and growth. While David needed minimal oxygen, Sam continued to need a moderate amount of Oxygen. Oxygen, while it is a lifesaver, can also have undesirable effects on the growing lungs, brain, and the delicate blood vessels of the retina- the inner lining of the eyes that receives light if given in excess. Hence, intense monitoring is needed by both non-invasive techniques and blood work. One of the consequences of frequent blood testing is the development of anemia, which then necessitates the need for a blood transfusion. Preterm babies have comparatively less volume of blood, and cumulatively, the small amount of blood collected for testing purposes and monitoring is enough for the babies to go anemic. Blood transfusion has its own set of problems that, again, must be carefully thought of in the care of these babies.

The few weeks past the first week of life are thus still perilous and test the expertise of the nursing and medical staff. While minimal handling and watchful expectancy is the aim of this period, in the life of these babies, it is still a period of great anxiety for the team. The act of treading on this path of what appears to be masterly inactivity is never to be taken lightly, as will be highlighted in the coming chapters.

Patent Ductus Arteriosus (PDA)

For Rosy and Rob, the next few days were relatively calm, but only to be informed on the morning round one day by the medical registrar that she heard a murmur overnight while listening to David's chest as a part of the examination. This often means the re-opening of a small blood vessel connecting the two great arteries, the pulmonary and the aorta, coming out of the heart from each of the ventricles – the right and left pumping chambers of the heart, respectively.

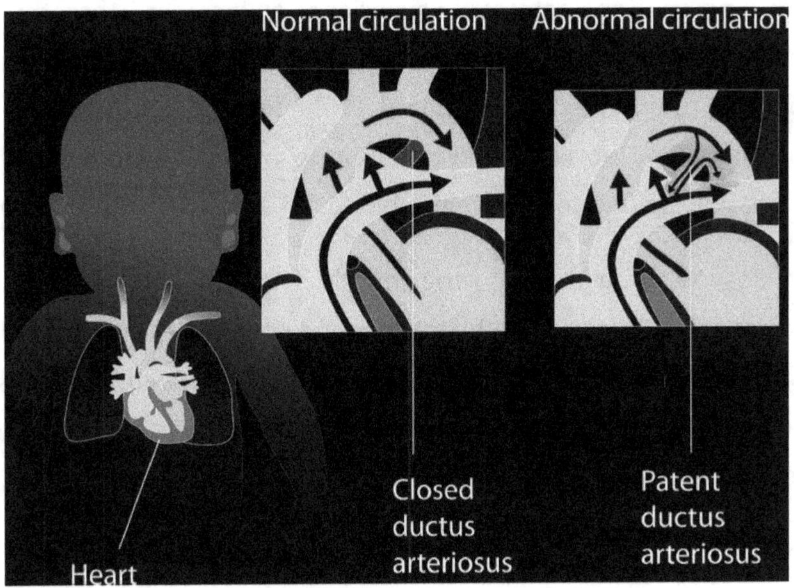

The patency of this blood vessel called ductus is essential for fetuses to survive inside the womb. It is necessary for the oxygenated blood coming from the placenta to bypass the lungs and send blood straight to the left side for circulation in the fetus. The lungs do not exchange gases in the blood when the baby is inside the womb. It is done by the placenta, which attaches the baby to the womb. Once the baby is born, this channel normally closes within a few hours as the gas exchange function is taken over by the lungs. However, in a significant number of very prematurely born infants, it can re-open, and this can give rise to a swishing sound (murmur) because of the turbulent flow of blood from the aorta (the main blood vessel taking the blood to the body) back to the pulmonary artery (the blood vessel from the heart taking the blood from the heart to the lungs) through this channel. Depending upon how much blood traverses back to the lungs, there can be consequences in the form of fluid overload in the lungs, and the baby could experience an increase in breathing effort and oxygen requirement. David, who was on minimal oxygen requirement, was noted to be needing more oxygen overnight and working harder to breathe, indicating that his lungs were getting flooded with extra blood.

Rosy was not there on the rounds, but Rob was told by the registrar overnight when he came in the evening. He deliberately decided to hold off telling Rosy, considering she was just recovering. He decided to come for the rounds in the morning to learn a bit more. Being a cardiologist in training and from his medical school days, he knew the consequences. He wanted to know the probabilities of the mischief that this new development could entail before talking to Rosy about it. Dr. Neil rattled off a few statistics from studies done in this area and surmised that the chances are high that this can worsen with time. Rob also wanted to know the threshold for doing something about it, and Dr. Neil told Rob that he needed to check the heart with an echocardiogram before he could give a better prediction. The

Echogram was already arranged to be done after the rounds, and he promised Rob that he would call and inform him once it was done.

The treatment of PDA has been a matter of debate amongst the specialists. There are several treatments available, including conservative management, medications, and surgery, each with its own benefits and risks. The fact that David needed more oxygen and an increase in respiratory support indicated that his lungs were now getting additional injuries and further inflammation that could lead to the need for prolonged respiratory support, called chronic lung disease (CLD). It could also have short-term consequences in the form of him using more energy for breathing and needing further improvement in his nutritional input. At the same time, it also made his gut not tolerate the milk and supplements because of an increased amount of gas escaping into his belly and the possibility of a decrease in blood flow due to the run-off blood from the left side to the right. PDA is a tricky situation, as you can imagine. An Echogram can estimate, to a certain extent, the size of the PDA and how much blood is flowing across the channel. This along with how David was coping, would help decide if anything more needed to be done.

Dr. Neil did the echocardiogram and confirmed that it was indeed the PDA that was the cause of the murmur. Occasionally, there can be some other reason for the murmur, so it was important to establish this fact first before going further. He estimated the size of the ductal vessel was moderate and that there was an increase in the flow across the channel. He called

Rob, but he deferred discussing anything further on the phone. Rob promised to come over that afternoon. Meanwhile, Dr. Neil ordered the team to hold feeds and cut down the volume of fluids being given to reduce the impact of the flooding in the lungs. He thought that David would need medical treatment sooner than later and wanted the parents to be aware of what it would involve and the benefits and harm that should be expected. Rob came in as promised in the afternoon, and Dr. Neil explained to him the Echo findings and his impression of the need to use medicine because he felt that the PDA could get bigger with time and cause more problems. By then, Rob had already done his own research and readily agreed to the plan. However, Dr. Neil informed him that Rosy needs to know, too, and he would not start the treatment till he hears from both the parents. Dr. Neil was particularly worried about the worsening feed intolerance but more worried about the increased risk of NEC that comes with a significant PDA. David was particularly prone to this, considering that he was stressed in utero and had shown decreased placental blood flow, which significantly reduces the flow of blood to the gut in order to divert the available blood to vital organs for immediate survival.

Rob could not agree more but was worried in how Rosy would take it. He decided to discuss it with her after work on returning home. Rosy was just beginning to feel a bit better from her depression, and Rob was concerned about her relapse. He decided to first touch base with her parents and wanted them to prepare her. But Rosy had already sensed that Rob was trying to hold off telling her something by the way he was behaving since coming home the previous evening after visiting NICU. Rob was unusually quieter than usual and appeared preoccupied. She had already decided to confront him. He called her parents and asked them to be around when he was back. They were waiting for him when he returned home, and Rosy knew that there was some bad news. She waited for Rob to settle down. Rob gently explained what was going on and how he thought it was important to use medicine to close the PDA in David. Rosy was expecting something worse and was a bit relieved that there was no disaster. She promptly agreed. She had been housebound for all these days but decided that now was the time for her to visit and be with their infants. She also wanted to check with Dr. Neil personally before consenting. Rob was happy, too, that Rosy was taking it better than he expected. So, that evening, after dinner, he took Rosy along to the hospital. Fortunately, Dr. Neil was on call and had come over for his evening rounds at 8 pm. He talked to them after his rounds, going through in more detail about the drug he thinks would work best and the expected benefit and risk. There are a few medications called NSAIDs (Non-Steroidal Anti-Inflammatory Agents) that could be used, and each with its own efficacy and risk. Dr. Neil decided to use Indomethacin. He was familiar with the drug, having been the first drug trialed for PDA, and was more confident of it working, although it was known to be less gentle to the gut than the other drugs available and being used in other parts of the world. Rob and Rosy trusted his judgment and were happy to go ahead.

The drug was given as per protocol in the unit. The baby was kept nil by mouth, and the prescribed monitoring was put in place. It worked; the murmur was no longer audible after two doses of the drug; an Echocardiogram done the next day confirmed the closure of PDA. The oxygen requirement and the breathing eased to a certain extent, and David appeared a bit more comfortable. However, the day after, David's urine output decreased markedly, and his abdomen started bloating again. Indomethacin is known to reduce urine output, and most clinicians believe that this is a temporary effect that indicates it is working as expected. The drug is also known to interfere with platelet (one of the components of blood that help with clotting of blood) function and reduce the number of platelets, which was again noted in David's blood. Neither abdominal distension nor low platelet level was anything unexpected. It just meant that David may need to remain off feeds for a while longer and continue monitoring his blood. Dr. Neil and the team were, however, concerned in view of the delicate nature of David's gut, which was deprived of adequate amounts of blood flow when he was in the womb for reasons mentioned before. An X-ray of the abdomen was ordered, which showed generalized distension of the intestines with gas but worryingly with gas within the bowel wall.

An ultrasound examination of the abdomen was also ordered, which showed some concerning features. There was decreased flow of blood to the kidneys, which accounted for the decreased urine output but what worried the team most was the finding of micro air bubbles in the blood vessels draining from the intestines.

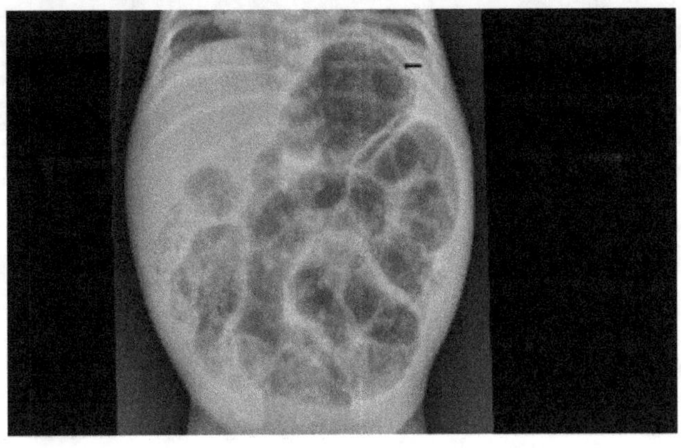

This was an indication of what could turn out to be the evolution of Necrotising Enterocolitis (NEC), the dreaded complication that Dr. Neil and his team were already concerned about. The pediatric surgical colleagues were consulted, and they reviewed the investigations with the radiology team. After examining the baby, they agreed that it could be in the initial stages of NEC. They advised caution and recommended treatment, which involved keeping the baby off feed for at least ten days, along with broad-spectrum antibiotics, pain relief, and regular surgical team review. All through this, the baby's nutrition had to be sustained through parenteral nutrition (nutrition through veins), and with it comes its own complications of liver dysfunction and infection, as mentioned before.

This was another setback that the parents had to deal with. To the medical team's relief, both Rosy and Rob took this in their stride and left the team to go with whatever was their best judgment. They were fully aware of what it meant from the earlier briefings that they had and were hoping for the best. The next few days were testing because, in addition to David's problems, Sam had ongoing concerns. He was still in need of moderately high levels of oxygen and respiratory support.

Necrotising Enterocolitis (NEC)

NEC is one of the most devastating diseases that a baby could get. If cancer is the emperor of all maladies in adults, NEC is the emperor of all the maladies known in preterm babies. It can kill in its most severe form, but even more dire is the suffering and pain in the acute stage with the potential for lifelong suffering from gut problems, growth, and development in the long term. Fortunately, most cases can be picked up early with diligent monitoring and prevented from going into their severe form by conservative medical management. When mild or moderate, it has the potential to recover fully, but in severe cases, varying lengths of the intestines get necrosed (die), needing the surgeons to go in and remove the dead gut. Depending on the length of the intestine involved, the surgeons will decide on the operating table the course of action, which may involve the removal of a small length and joining back the rest or to create a diversional stoma (an opening onto the surface of the abdomen) of the proximal healthy part and leaving the rest to heal within. Rarely, they may resort to removing large chunks of the affected bowel, leading eventually to a condition called the short gut syndrome. It will then need multiple gut surgeries in the future and sometimes intestinal transplants. Occasionally, the surgeons may decide after opening the abdomen not to do anything because of the extensive nature of intestinal damage that will eventually lead to the demise of the baby.

Unfortunately for Rosy and Rob, David's gut problems got worse over the days. His abdominal distension worsened, and the skin over his abdomen started turning red and tender with inflammation. His respiratory support requirement rapidly increased, and he had to be intubated again and put on the breathing machine. His condition deteriorated further and reached a point where the pediatric surgeons decided that they needed to operate. A meeting was set up between the parents and the surgeon, Mr. Adnan, his team, the medical team, and the social worker, Ms. Lorraine. The team explained all the necessary details of the status of the disease process, and consent was sought. Rosy started crying and became inconsolable, and Rob was very worried as well. They knew that they had no choice but to go with the medical opinion and hope for the best. After the surgeons left, they sought some time for themselves to gather their thoughts. Ms Lorraine volunteered to stay, but they wanted to be left alone. Rob realized that it would be better for Rosy to have her parents by her side and informed them to come over. It is at times like this that your faith in God is tested. He suggested, to Rosy's surprise, that it would be nice for them to meet with the hospital chaplain and seek solace. He decided to go back to his ward and immerse himself in work to take his mind off while Rosy, with her parents, went to the church to pray. They both decided to return in a few hours for the surgery.

The operation was organized for that afternoon. The anesthetists met with them soon after they returned and obtained their consent, explaining in detail the process and requesting them to be available for further discussions through the surgical process. The medical team meanwhile arranged to transport the baby to the operating theatre. Rosy and Rob accompanied the medical team to the theatre and decided to remain in the lobby. Dr. Neil accompanied the team into the operating theatre to assist in decision-making and to communicate with the parents, who were waiting outside the theatre.

In modern medical practice, it is imperative that every possible outcome is explained to the family, in as much detail as the family desires to know, before any procedure. Being medical graduates themselves, Rosy and Rob were aware of the spectrum of the outcome but were still interested in knowing the probabilities of the worst. It is human nature to worry about the worst. The very fact that David had to be taken to the theatre was itself a matter of grave concern. The worst outcome in theatre could be death on the table. Fortunately, with the advancement of medical practice, state-of-the-art anesthetic expertise, and the availability of intensive care options, this outcome is extremely rare. Unfortunately, though, this sometimes comes with the sad situation of prolonging life. Dr. Neil wanted to be around to help make decisions, and the parents greatly appreciated this.

It takes a while to move a sick baby from the transport incubator onto the table for operation. Dr. Neil was relieved to know that Dr. Wright was the anesthetist. Over the years, they had formed a great bond and trusted each other. The anesthetists are acutely aware of sudden destabilization during this process. They make sure that the process follows a practiced sequence, and once the baby is moved, they take time to make sure that there are enough devices attached to monitor the vital signs and lines inserted to access blood sampling and fluid administration.

Dr Wright was a master in his art and went about his craft in an expeditious way. David was on a significant number of medications for pain control and for maintaining heart function, including blood pressure. He was already intubated and continued to be artificially ventilated; blood products were ordered and available for emergency transfusion. Mr. Adnan and his assistant, Mr. Selvam, waited for the signal to start from Dr. Wright. They quickly draped the abdomen of David with sterile surgical sheets and, on the nod from the anesthetist, went about the delicate process of the operation. The moment the abdominal cavity was opened, the foul smell of the dead intestine wafted into the air, and there was an audible gasp from the team. It indicated the possibility of the worst scene to follow. There was hardly anything said, but as Mr. Adnan proceeded further to explore the abdomen, it became clear from the nod of his head that they were heading for a disaster. Foul-smelling fluid mixed with blood and pus emanated from the surgical wound, confirming that the intestine had perforated. The peritoneum, the membrane that covers the intestines and lines the interior of the abdomen, was soiled with the contents of the bowel. Mr. Adnan delicately lifted a portion of the intestine for everyone to see. It was pale grey and had multiple perforations(holes). Further examination revealed that almost the entire length of the small intestine was essentially dead and non-salvageable. A palpable pall of doom and gloom could be felt in the room. Mr. Adnan briefly talked about not doing anything further and looked at Dr. Neil. This meant that the abdomen would be closed without any further intervention, and the baby returned to the NICU for palliative care. Dr. Neil nodded in agreement and took a deep breath. He now had the responsibility of communicating the devastating news with the family and making them understand that it was in the best interest of the baby, the parents, and the family to let the baby pass away. He was contemplating how to deal with questions from parents regarding the future steps. He had earlier explained to the parents about the remote possibility of sustaining life with no intestine and the future gut transplant, but in his mind, he was clear that this would not be the best option in the current situation, considering how small David was and how arduous that path would be to tread, for the family.

Palliative Care in NICU

Much of neonatal ethical decision-making revolves around the limits of viability. The newborn stage of life at any gestational level is one of the most vulnerable periods in the life of a human being. Newborns are generally quite resilient, but despite the resilience that we often see amongst newborns, it does not take much to upset the apple cart and the baby getting on to life support. With the advancement of intensive care, it is easy to play God and sustain life at all costs. In the NICU, neonatal practitioners constantly face the ethical issue of when to let go. It takes a lot of experience and understanding to counsel parents and families to help them make pragmatic and acceptable decisions for them to move on, and sometimes, it involves helping them to let go. Unlike in adult age groups, in intensive care settings, pediatricians and neonatologists do not have the individual patient's tacit desire or instructions to go by. The parents and/or the guardians must always make that call, and therefore, it behooves them to be fully informed so that they can agree with the physician's opinion. It is also a delicate task for the doctors, and often, their own judgment may not align with the family's wishes. The fundamental reason one chooses to become a doctor is to cure and save; therefore, asking families to limit care or withdraw support is a heavy burden for them as well that the families may not understand. Consequently, it is imperative that trust is established between the family and the treating doctor. Thankfully, a specialty called palliative care is emerging where people, not necessarily doctors, with expertise in dealing with death and dying and knowledge of bioethics and laws are available in most of the so-called developed world. Yet, it will remain the prime responsibility of the responsible physician to initiate these discussions with the families before palliative care specialists can take over. There are often guidelines based on evidence to go by, but there is still a requirement for the physician to exert judgment. And then, there is this conflict in ethics between the autonomy of the patient and justice for society. Intensive care is a very expensive business in health care, and often, it is the combined resources of the society that are subsidized to meet this expense. As mentioned before, one can sustain life at all costs for prolonged periods in intensive care, but in hopeless situations, it takes a lot of emotional suffering on the part of the family to let go. The families often would not realize that the doctor is also undergoing emotional drain in coming to terms with a decision to let go. Fortunately, almost always, it is a team decision, but it remains a delicate task for the lead doctor to convince the families to go for the palliative care option. It usually takes time and may require multiple sittings with the families and their support system to get them to agree with the medical team's opinion. Most families will understand and eventually agree, but occasionally, it may take the legal systems to come into play, often with bitter consequences for everyone involved on both sides.

Rob was startled when he received the call from Dr. Neil from the operation theatre. He had gone into a meditative mood and was not thinking of anything specific, while Rosy remained alert and was praying. From the tone of Dr. Neil's voice, Rob realized that some bad news was about to be given. He half thought of cutting short the conversation, but Rosy was staring at him and looked very eager to hear from Dr. Neil. She almost grabbed the phone from Rob's hand in a reflexive move and asked if everything was OK. Dr. Neil told them that he wanted to talk to them in person urgently as he started walking his way out of the theatre. Dr. Neil did not want to convey such big news on the phone. He found both Rob and Rosy eagerly waiting as he arrived. They could see from the seriousness of his face that they were going to hear some very bad news. They had no time to brace as Dr. Neil ushered them into a side room for privacy. As he moved by, he grabbed a tissue box, expecting Rosy to break down. He started off in a calm and composed voice as they settled into their respective chairs. He wasted no time explaining what Mr. Adnan found on the table and what it meant. He told them that Mr. Adnan had decided not to go further, considering that this was not a salvageable situation, and that he agreed. Rosy was heartbroken and burst out crying as Dr. Neil pushed the tissue box towards her. Rob asked if a gut transplant was still a viable option here, half expecting that it would not be. Dr. Neil did not answer the question straight away but outlined what it would involve, insisting on the pain and suffering that the baby would go through if they decided to go for that option. He told them that considering how premature and delicate David was, it would not guarantee success at the end of all the suffering. Both Rosy and Rob agreed by nodding their heads. Dr. Neil then waited for a moment for both to regain their composure and then outlined what the next steps of the palliative option would be. He then left them to reflect and contemplate and went back into the OT.

By then, Mr. Adnan had already closed the abdomen, and Dr. Wright had called for the orderly to come in to take David back to the NICU. As the NICU team emerged back from the theatre with David in the incubator, Dr. Neil asked them to wait in the lobby as he briskly walked to the room where he had left Rosy and Rob. They both got up from their seats as soon as Dr. Neil walked in, expecting further news, but Dr. Neil gently asked them to accompany him to the lobby where the NICU team was waiting. After the parents had a brief time with their baby, the team proceeded to the NICU. Everyone was silent as they walked the corridors to the NICU. On arrival at the NICU, Dr. Neil waited for the team to settle the baby back into the crib and then called Rob aside to tell him that Mr. Adnan would be in soon to talk to them. At the same time, he asked Rob if they would like the grandparents and any other support person to be around for a briefing. Rob said he would discuss it with Rosy and come back.

The meeting occurred a couple of hours after David was brought back from the theatre. Both Rosy and Rob did not want their parents or any other support person. They agreed that Ms. Lorraine, the social worker, should be around. After the routine introductions, Mr. Adnan explained the findings during the operations and why he concluded that the intestines were unsalvageable. Dr. Neil then explained what that meant for the baby in greater detail. Rosy kept sobbing while Rob asked some real practical questions again concerning the possibility of prolonging David's life by continuing with life support and parenteral nutrition until he was big enough for a gut transplant. Dr. Neil stated that it is possible to sustain David on long-term TPN

(Total Parenteral Nutrition), but he explained that it would involve many challenges, like the need for a central venous line and the possibility of infection. He also talked about its effect on his liver; prolonged TPN can damage liver function and, ultimately, liver failure, although this has become less of a problem with advanced TPN practices. Then there was the bigger question of home TPN for a prolonged period till David would be ready for the transplant, if and when a suitable donor could be found. Meanwhile, he insisted that they would have to not only be patient but also understand the pain and agony of the process, besides the quality of life during and beyond the waiting period, and how it will affect not only David but Sam and them as a family unit. The fact that David had already had grade III bleeding in the brain and with the additional stress of multiple surgeries, exposure to anesthetic agents that come with it, and prolonged pain relief medications, all would have an adverse impact on his cognitive outcome as well if he survives the ordeal.

Intensive care is not all about survival; the major impact on the quality of life of not only the individual but also his immediate and extended family must be factored into decision-making. Although survival rates have significantly improved in the last few years, the improvement in the quality of life of survivors and its adverse effects have not kept pace. With more and more extreme preterm babies surviving, the burden of individuals with handicaps has only increased.

There are often three choices for the parents to consider- First, continuing with life support indefinitely. Second, no further escalation of support, meaning if David deteriorated further while on life support due to any reason, then not go for any heroic measures like cardiac massage and further medications or, third, immediate withdrawal of support. Dr. Neil briefly outlined what each step of those choices would entail and how it will be executed but told them that the details can be discussed later after they had made up their mind.

Decisions impacting life and death are some of the biggest that the families and the medical teams have to take regularly in intensive care setups. It remains the responsibility of the medical team and its leadership to lay out all the realistic scenarios based on evidence and help guide the families. Although the final decision remains the responsibility of the family, the medical team should take the lead to guide and help. There is a fine yet thin line that separates paternalism from independent choice, and the medical team should be aware of the risk of transgressing that line because of its ethical implications and its effect on the parents in the long term because, after all, it is the parents who will have to live with the consequences. It is important that the families are not rushed into such situations. Many factors from the individual parents come into play. Their individual understanding and viewpoints based on their faith and circumstances must all be considered.

So, the family was then left to reflect and deliberate. The social worker caught up with them again about the various support services available, including the possibility of organizing a larger family meeting with the rest of the family and their trusted friends. They were reassured that till such time they make up their minds, all measures of life support, including pain relief, will be continued.

Rob had no doubt in his mind that he would not want any more suffering for his son, and in the end, if it was a situation where David would continue to need surgeries and medical attention throughout the rest of his life, he was clear that he would opt for withdrawal of support and help David pass away in peace. He was not certain, though, that Rosy would be on the same page given her faith and expressed opinion on the sanctity of life. Rosy, on the other hand, was aware of what Rob was thinking. She knew that he was practical and would make the right decision. She wanted time to clear her mind and discuss this with both their parents. Rob was happy to go with this and arranged for his parents to come over. They arrived the next day and went to the hospital with Rosy's parents. They were apprised of the need to make this ethical decision when Rob called them to come in. Both their parents had discussed their viewpoints and had come to the decision that it would be best for them to support Rosy and Rob in whatever they opt to do. Meanwhile, Rob let Rosy do her own thinking and was pleasantly surprised when she eventually came to terms with the thought that further suffering for David would not be in anybody's interest. She was very sad, but they finally agreed to withdraw further care.

When parents are faced with the heart-wrenching decision to withdraw life support for their baby in the Newborn Intensive Care Unit (NICU), their emotional landscape becomes a tumultuous sea of grief, love, and impossible choices. This moment shrouded in a profound sense of loss and helplessness, is one of the most devastating experiences a parent can endure. The first reaction is often shock and disbelief. They cling to hope, especially a mother who is unable to comprehend that the tiny life she nurtured inside her and held with such tenderness might not survive. Despite the medical explanations and the grim prognosis, there is a part of her that desperately hopes for a miracle. This denial serves as a temporary shield against the overwhelming reality.

As the gravity of the situation sinks in, grief envelops them. This grief is not just for the baby they might lose but for the future they will never share—the first steps, first words, birthdays, and all the moments they had envisioned. It is a profound sense of loss for a life that was just beginning. Every touch, every breath the baby takes feels like a fleeting treasure, intensifying the pain.

Guilt often follows closely. A mother may question her actions, her decisions during pregnancy, and her ability to protect her baby. The "what ifs" and "if only's" plague her thoughts despite knowing rationally that she did everything she could. Self-doubt gnaws at her, and she grapples with the tormenting question of whether there was anything else she could have done.

The decision to withdraw life support is an agonizing one. It involves weighing the baby's quality of life against the medical interventions keeping them alive. They must consider whether continuing treatment would cause more suffering than relief. This decision feels like a monumental burden, as it goes against every instinct to protect and nurture. During this time, they need immense support and understanding from family, friends, and healthcare professionals. They require a space to express their emotions, to cry, to rage, and to grieve without judgment. Compassionate communication from doctors, nurses, and other support staff, who can explain the medical realities with empathy, is crucial.

When the decision is made, they face the unbearable task of saying goodbye. The mother holds her baby close, imprinting every detail in her memory. The moments become sacred—each touch, each whispered word, a testament to her love. This farewell is both an ending and a beginning, marking the transition from life to memory.

Once the decision was made, Rob and Rosy informed the medical team that they would like to have a meeting soon to declare their option. A meeting was arranged expeditiously, and to everyone's relief, the decision was made. Dr. Neil and the Nurse in charge of that shift, along with Ms. Lorraine, the social worker, then explained the process to the family. The plan was to move David into Rosy's room in the NICU, where she had been staying since the operation, continue pain relief, and wean off the rest of life support while Rosy held David in her arms. She requested that the hospital priest be present along with both of their parents. The priest offered a brief prayer after David was removed from the incubator and placed in Rosy's arms; Rob sat close by. David did not last long after the breathing tube was removed and passed away peacefully.

In the aftermath, parents often embark on a long and arduous journey of healing. Grief does not follow a linear path; it ebbs and flows, sometimes overwhelming, sometimes quietly present. They may seek solace in support groups, therapy, or spiritual practices. Over time, they learn to carry the memory of their baby with a tender balance of sorrow and love.

Through this profound experience, the parents discover the depths of their strength and the boundless capacity of their hearts. Their perspective on life, love, and loss is forever changed. While the pain remains a part of them, so does the love they feel for their baby—a love that, even in the face of such profound loss, shines with an unyielding light.

Ongoing Care for the
surviving Twin

Grieving is going to be a lifelong process for the loss of your near and dear ones. Swiss-American psychiatrist Elisabeth Kubler-Ross is famous for outlining the five stages of grief — denial, anger, bargaining, depression, and acceptance — and wrote, "These are a part of the framework that makes up our learning to live without the one we lost." It is important to mention here that not all individuals go through all five stages. It all depends on one's own mental status, beliefs, faiths, understanding, and support systems. However, to move on in life and get closure, one needs to come to some sort of acceptance; the sooner it happens, the better.

The loss of a baby in the Newborn Intensive Care Unit (NICU) is a devastating experience for parents. The emotions they go through are complex and profound. Initially, there is often a sense of shock and disbelief. Even when the outcome is expected due to the baby's condition, the finality of death can be difficult to comprehend. Parents may feel numb and unable to process the reality of their loss. As the shock wears off, overwhelming grief sets in. This grief is not just for the loss of a baby but for all the dreams and hopes they had for their child's future. Every milestone they anticipated, from first steps to first words, becomes a painful reminder of what will never be.

Guilt and self-blame are common emotions. Parents may question everything they did or didn't do during pregnancy and their baby's time in the NICU. They might wonder if there was something they could have done differently to change the outcome, even if, rationally, they know they did everything possible.

Anger can also surface—anger at the situation, at the medical team, or even at themselves. This anger can be a way to cope with the intense pain and helplessness they feel. Frustration about the inability to protect their child and the loss of control over their lives is a powerful emotion.

The sorrow and longing for their baby can be all-consuming. Parents might replay moments with their baby, cherishing every touch and look while longing for more time. The absence of their baby is felt deeply and poignantly in every corner of their lives. There's often a sense of isolation and loneliness, even when surrounded by supportive family and friends. Others may struggle to understand the depth of their loss, leading parents to feel disconnected and alone in their grief.

Many parents go through a period of searching for meaning, trying to make sense of their loss. This might involve spiritual or religious exploration or simply a search for a way to honor their baby's memory and make their brief life significant. Despite the isolation, the need for support and connection is crucial. Parents may find solace in support groups, counseling, or connecting with other parents who have experienced similar losses. Sharing their story and being heard can be a vital part of the healing process.

Acceptance and healing are gradual and ongoing. The pain never fully goes away, but with time, parents learn to carry their grief and integrate it into their lives. The love they have for their baby remains, becoming a part of who they are and how they move forward.

Through the darkness, parents often discover an inner resilience and strength they never knew they had. The journey of grief is arduous, but it can also reveal the boundless capacity for love and the ability to endure even the most profound loss. This insight captures the emotional turmoil and journey that parents may experience after losing a baby in the NICU. Every parent's journey is unique, but the shared experience of profound love and loss binds them together.

Every day that Samson is in the intensive care unit, the fear of the same happening to him will weigh on Rosy, Rob, and their family members. The risk of death is an ever-present consequence in NICU. This realization was not lost on them. It took a few days for them to open up and ask about Samson, how he was doing, and where he was heading.

It was difficult to say if their trust in the medical team was dented, but their anxiety was palpable. Fortunately, Samson continued to remain in a fairly stable state, although he needed a moderate amount of oxygen and assistance to breathe. What was worrying to the medical team was his nutrition. With the ongoing need for respiratory support also comes the requirement for more nutrition. Rosy's dwindling breast milk supply was only compounded by the inability to add human milk fortifiers, which was stopped when David took a bad turn. This meant supplementing him with formula milk or prolonging his parenteral nutrition; both have their unique risks. The other option would be to use donated human milk.

Donor milk is now available in most neonatal units. These are pooled donor samples that are then screened and pasteurized. There is an inherent problem with this process because it would be different from the composition of the mother's own milk. The milk composition is known to vary from individual-to-individual mothers, depending upon the gestation and age of the baby, and is thus unique to the needs of the mother's own baby. It is also known to vary in composition in relation to the time of the day it is expressed. Besides, the donor human milk supplied from the milk banks loses the protective factors that come with fresh human milk because of the processing involving pasteurization, though it is much safer from the risk of infection. There is still a need to add human milk fortifiers or individual supplements to cover the deficiencies that it comes with. Nevertheless, it is still considered to be the next best option.

However, Waikato hospital did not have a dedicated milk bank at that time and was dependent on other lactating mothers who had excess milk supply to contribute. Rosy and Robert were happy for the team to use donor milk, thus procured if available, even though not processed through a milk bank. They were then apprised of the process that existed then, with the issues regarding screening for possible viruses like the HIV (Human Immunodeficiency Virus), HTLVs (Human T cell Lymphotropic Viruses), and CMV (Cytomegalovirus), the risk of bacterial contamination, and the need for mutual consent from both donee and donor mothers. They were fortunate and grateful to have willing donor mothers in the unit and were prepared to accept the risks.

While the feeding and weight gain issues were being addressed, the team was also planning strategies to reduce the risks of diseases like Chronic Lung Disease (CLD) and Retinopathy of prematurity (ROP). CLD, as mentioned before, is a debilitating consequence of being subjected to artificial respiratory support depending upon how severe the disease process is, from mild to severe. It induces inflammation that continues as long as the support is continued. Besides, it goes through a process of healing with scar formation and compensatory adjustments of the volume of the air sacs happening simultaneously from the waxing and waning nature of the body's response. This results in alteration of the architecture of the lungs as well. There are several strategies available for CLD prevention, each with its own unique benefits and risks. On the other hand, ROP is a disease with the potential to cause varying degrees of damage to the retina (the membrane at the back of the eyes where the incoming light from the eyes falls). This can lead to impairment of vision and in severe cases, even blindness. Excess oxygen traversing through the blood vessels of the retina is believed to cause the proliferation of the blood vessels in the developing retina of very premature babies and these new blood vessels tend to bleed and rarely, lead to detachment of the membrane of the retina in severe cases.

It was already nearing three weeks, and the neonatal team was concerned about Samson's ongoing need for respiratory support and oxygen requirement. Dr. Neil decided to meet with the parents to update them about the ongoing concerns and to explain the various strategies that could be used with their own potential risks and benefits. Despite being doctors or because of being doctors with some knowledge of these potential problems, they were very anxious. However, they felt resigned to their fate and decided to let Dr. Neil and the team do their best as per their clinical judgment and experience after having heard from the team.

CLD and ROP are additional factors that are known to adversely affect long-term neurodevelopmental outcomes as well, besides the specific organ-related morbidities mentioned before. The damaged lung has the capacity to repair and regrow, but in a significant number of survivors, CLD will continue to remain a lifelong issue going into late adulthood, as per recent follow-up data. Adult physicians and respiratory care specialists are just beginning to see an increasing number of long-term survivors of prematurity seeking treatment and advice for lung-related problems. The best strategy would be prevention or at least limiting the damage to the lungs. A lot of neonatal specialists and scientists are currently involved in research to find ways to prevent CLD. Besides the oxygen toxicity and artificial respiratory support, the researchers have identified trigger factors starting as early as when the babies are still in the womb. They have realized that there is no single strategy that may be enough and are now engaged in multi-pronged strategies based on emerging evidence like prevention of infection, use of steroids in threatened premature births, non-invasive respiratory supports, early use of artificial surfactants, intense and rigorous monitoring of oxygen needs, etc. Despite this, a significant number of babies still develop CLD of varying severity. The worst affected are the smallest premature babies; the smaller they are, the greater the risk. Once CLD is set in, the next strategy would be to restrict further damage using some of the same principles mentioned, along with the use of anti-inflammatory medications like steroids. The most potent steroid medication currently being used is Dexamethasone. Its use has a chequered story of itself. Being a very potent anti-inflammatory medication, it has the potential to restrict the natural growth of body cells, particularly the brain cells. The neonatal community learned about these negative effects in the mid-nineties when they started seeing an increased incidence of cerebral palsies in babies where it was used liberally. So, great caution must be exercised. The dosages used have been significantly scaled down now, but scientists and doctors are still not sure of the exact doses required and the duration needed to get the optimal benefit while aiming to limit harm. This remains a hot topic of research and scientific deliberations currently. Obviously, the best approach should be individualized. With the arrival of artificial intelligence and precision medicine, one hopes that the days are not too far before one can get the best individualized treatment, not only for neonatal problems but for all the myriads of disease processes affecting mankind at all age groups.

Retinopathy of Prematurity

Retinopathy of Prematurity, or ROP as it is generally called in practice, is the classic example of the dictum, which states that 'just because an intervention is good, does not imply that more of it is better.' The field of neonatal medicine is littered with many practices that have caused harm because of over-enthusiastic use of interventions that showed benefit initially. The use of excess oxygen was one such. In the middle of the last century, doctors and scientists discovered that oxygen use is a double-edged sword. While it is a life savior, it also has the potential for bodily harm if used excessively.

The brunt of its adverse effects is mainly borne by the brain, the eyes, and the lungs. Excess oxygen releases free radicals that evoke inflammation in these organs with disastrous consequences. In the brain, it causes damage, resulting in long-term neuro-developmental deficits, especially in preterm babies. We also know now that it is a big contributor to the brain damage caused in term and near-term babies who suffer asphyxia at birth. In the eyes of premature babies, whose retina (the membrane that receives light) is not yet mature, it results in the proliferation of blood vessels, resulting in bleeding and, in severe cases, a detachment that can cause visual abnormalities that lead to blindness. The famous American blind singer-songwriter and musician, Stevie Wonder is one of the high-profile victims of blindness due to ROP. In the lungs, as mentioned previously, it is one of the causes of ongoing inflammation that leads to CLD and, paradoxically, oxygen dependency with all its long-term consequences, as described in the last chapter.

It is important to monitor for the early signs of ROP. It generally starts appearing at about 30- 32 weeks. The earlier it is picked up, the better the chance of limiting the damage. Most units would have specialized pediatric ophthalmologists and equipment to screen for ROP.

Samson, the surviving twin, was at high risk for developing ROP because of his ongoing dependence on moderate amounts of oxygen. He was already about six weeks old, nearing the time for screening. The neonatal team had booked him for Dr. Brown, the visiting Pediatric Ophthalmologist, to screen. The screening involves putting certain eye drops to dilate the pupils (the small pinhole openings in each eye through which light travels into the eye); it takes a few hours to start working. The process of examination itself is quite stressful because the ophthalmologist uses instruments to stop the eyes from moving and requires the nursing staff to restrain the baby from moving. Although the examination itself only takes about a few minutes, it is intense enough to upset and destabilize the baby. For this reason, most units would discourage the families from being around to witness this process. The combination of the eyedrops and the stress of examination have been found to be associated with problems of apnoea (stoppage of breathing), bradycardia (slowing of heart rate), hypoxia (low oxygen level in the blood), swings in blood pressure, feed intolerance and in some cases NEC. Yet again, it highlights the delicate path that neonatal teams must tread in the care of premature babies. This being the case, the team takes informed consent and usually would arrange for a meeting with the family to explain the process.

Dr. Neil had called in the parents for a meeting. Only Rosy could make it. She knew to some extent what it involved and was happy to inform Rob. Rob was tied up with his work at the hospital. Rosy decided to get her parents to be with her when Dr. Neil spoke with her. As usual, Dr. Neil started off by asking Rosy about how much she knew about the process and its consequences. She was certainly not aware that the process could possibly destabilize Sam. He was just about stable and beginning to show some signs of wellness. The thought of the possibility of feed intolerance and NEC frightened her the most. She grew very anxious, and tears started welling in her eyes. Dr. Neil stopped and tried to reassure her that the chances of that happening were very slim, but how do you convince a mother who had already lost one child? He decided to give her some time and space to recover and left the room. Rosy was consoled by her parents. They convinced her to keep faith in God and leave it all to the team to do what is necessary.

Thereafter, as planned, the examination took place at the appointed time. It was no surprise to the neonatal team when Dr. Brown found that Samson had bilateral stage III ROP, meaning significant changes in the retina as evidenced by a ridge separating the vascularised zone (area with blood vessels) from the peripheral avascularised zone (area devoid of blood vessels). There were also areas of inflammation and proliferation of blood vessels, which makes it a 'plus disease' indicating the need for therapy soon.

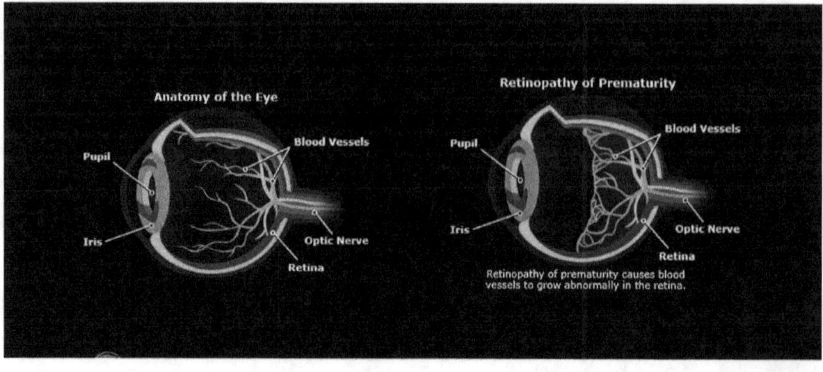

The various therapeutic options or management of ROP have evolved over the years. It has come a long way from the use of Cryo (freezing) to Laser photocoagulation to the latest use of site and disease-specific antibody called Avastin. Rosy and Rob, when told by Dr Brown, were disappointed to know this but showed few emotions having resigned to their fate. They were however relieved that the process itself did not disturb Samson much. Dr. Brown explained to them the need to go for therapy and what it involves. It was decided that Samson would best benefit from Laser therapy, for which he would need to go to the operation theatre. Laser therapy involves shooting pulses of laser beam to the affected areas in the retina. In a typical session, thousands of beams are shot over a short period of time. It is painful and would need anesthesia.

Thankfully, the procedure went smoothly. General anesthesia was not used, but under controlled conditions of the OT, the anesthetist decided to use the drug dexmedetomidine (Dexmet), which Dr. Neil had suggested. This drug brings about a dissociative effect, in the sense the individual often does not experience the pain and discomfort, thus making the procedure less destabilizing. It is important to mention here, though, that its use is not widely researched for use in newborn medicine, just like many other practices that have crept into this specialty. The next few days involved careful monitoring for any side effects of the drug used and aftereffects of the procedure. Dr. Brown planned for a review examination to be done the week after. Often, one such procedure is all that is required in expert hands; however, the life journey of a premature baby is such that nothing can be taken for granted.

Fortunately, everything went smoothly, to the great relief of everyone involved. It was now time to focus on the next steps to help Samson grow and develop while steadily being weaned off technology that he was still dependent on. He was still on non-invasive respiratory support in the form of CPAP, still needing a moderate amount of oxygen and medications to help him breathe. He was still on tube feeds and various supplements. The team was focused on keeping him safe from hospital-borne infections and watchful of various organ-related dysfunctions that he was still at risk for. To their disadvantage, he was still a few weeks away from nearing the expected date of discharge home, which generally would be expected to be around the time he would have been born if premature delivery had not happened, that is, around the 40th week of gestation. It is rare for preterm-born babies to be ready for discharge around that time, but neonatal physicians would generally hope and work towards this point in the life of a preterm baby. A point in time also gives the parents time to focus, but the team would go out of their way to ground them to their realities while trying to keep their hopes up.

Chronic Lung Disease

Chronic Lung Disease (CLD), also called Bronchopulmonary Dysplasia (BPD) or Northway's Disease after the pathologist from Stanford University College of Medicine, who described it (because of damage to the airway and the lungs) as the name suggests, a chronic problem involving the lungs. CLD/BPD is seen in a significant proportion of preterm babies born at or before the gestational age of 32 weeks. The more premature the baby at birth, the greater the risk and the severity. It is a disease process brought about by the damages done to the immature lungs from oxygen use, invasive artificial breathing support, infection, and alteration in the developmental process of the lungs that comes with being born prematurely. The underlying pathology is inflammation, as mentioned before, and healing with scar formation within the lungs, leading to the alteration in the whole lung architecture that comes with it. It is yet not well understood as to why some preterm babies escape. There may be genetic components playing a role, too. Medical science has used many multimodal approaches to prevent and/or treat while helping the lungs to grow as normally in a baby not affected by the process, with good nutrition also playing an important role. Many of the approaches involve the use of prenatal steroids in threatened preterm delivery, limiting oxygen use for resuscitation and subsequent care, avoiding or restrictive use of invasive artificial breathing support, use of surfactants early in susceptible babies, and anti-inflammatory agents such as steroids. Some recent research is looking at the use of stem cells early in the healing stage to help grow normal lung tissue. CLD is known to affect not only lung-related problems but has been found to affect neurodevelopment as well. Some lung-related problems can affect individuals going into adulthood and later may reduce their quality of life and longevity. It, therefore, remains one of the most important issues in the neonatal practice, especially in the effort to improve the quality of life in the survivors of premature births.

For Samson, the dependence on oxygen and CPAP, in addition to his reaching the stage to begin the process of suckle feeding, had been the focus of discussion with his parents following his recovery process from ROP. Rosy and Rob were updated frequently by the team about the next strategies being used and the pros and cons of those strategies. They were aware that, at some stage, the team would consider the use of steroids to limit the inflammation. Steroids, as mentioned earlier, are like a double-edged sword with benefits when used judiciously but also harm in the form of stopping the growth of new lung tissue at least temporarily while being used and the potential for increasing the risk of cerebral palsy and poor neurodevelopmental outcome. The team decided first to give Samson a chance to improve his weight by encouraging optimal nutrition while getting him to wean off the tube feeds. One of the strategies used was to switch over from CPAP to a high-flow oxygen air mixture through a nasal cannula while carefully titrating the need for oxygen. The high-flow nasal cannula approach, again, is the result of a few years of research suggesting that it can be an alternative method for respiratory support. This approach may not be better than CPAP, but at least the studies show that it may be non-inferior. The advantage is taking off nasal prongs and facilitating breastfeeding. Most parents and nursing staff tend to like this because of the ease of handling the baby and its obvious benefit of helping foster bonding with the baby besides helping with breastfeeding. The Waikato newborn unit had adopted a cue-based feeding approach that facilitated breastfeeding. This involves the mother being around and trying to suckle feed from the breast when the baby shows signs of needing a feed. It is both an exciting and occasionally frustrating period for parents. Rosy and Rob were aware of the importance of breast milk and were excited to contribute to the process. They saw progress and realized the possibility of them being more involved in Samson's care. Simultaneously, the team discussed with the dietary specialist how to optimize the calorie and protein input to facilitate appropriate growth.

The next phase of care would go on for at least the next 4-6 weeks. Generally, during this phase, babies are moved to a lesser level of care (level II) from intensive care (level III). This is a big moment for the families as they start seeing, as they say, 'light at the end of the tunnel.' Incidentally, transferring from Level III to Level II could also be terrifying for a first-time parent, as the intensity of medical/nursing attention is scaled down. The one-to-one care that the parents got used to is now reduced and parents are coached to be more involved in the care of their babies. Mother Craft, as it is called, is a unique skill that first-time parents have to learn. With the additional burden of their baby being fragile, this could be stressful and often goes unrecognized by the healthcare staff. This period is the beginning of the preparation for eventual discharge home. Rosy had been continuing with the expression of milk as advised by the lactation consultant, and for her, it was the actual moment when her maternal role was kicking in. Rob, as usual, was very supportive and began to spend more time in the unit despite his busy training schedule. Rosy was beginning to feel better from her mental health point of view, and that helped with the lactation as well. She began to eat well and sleep longer periods undisturbed.

Fortunately, this phase passes fast for the families as most members start seeing hope and positive vibes. The delicate balance can, however, tilt to periods of anxiety if the progress is stalled or interrupted by complications. A lot of patience and compassion is required to get the families to go through this phase. Success in this phase is dependent on many factors: increasing parental involvement, nursing expertise, understanding, and confidence building play a very big role, too. The expectation from the team is to get the baby to grow appropriately, and with growth, the dependence on technology decreases. Samson started growing reasonably well, and his ability to suckle feed improved over time. His oxygen requirement, however, showed minimal reduction to the dissatisfaction of the team. He, however, was exerting less effort while trying to breathe, a sign that his physical dependence may come down eventually. The possibility of the need to use steroids remained an option. His follow up X-ray chest was showing signs of moderate CLD.

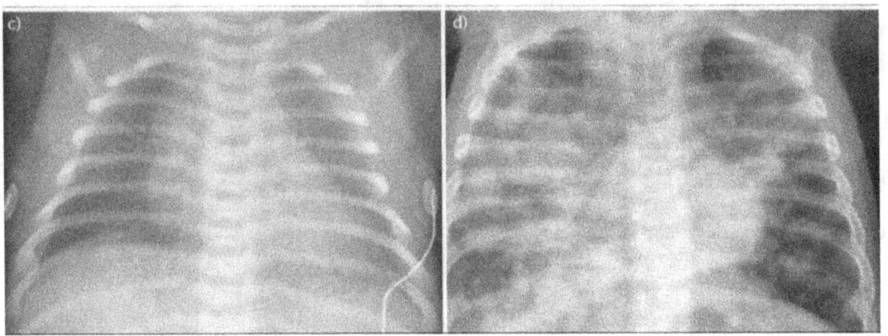

Chest X-Ray: Normal lung vs. Lung with CLD

Samson would continue to remain on a high-flow nasal oxygen air mixture till he is at least 36 weeks corrected for prematurity and beyond. At this stage, the team would be thinking of possible discharge in the next few weeks, but they would like to see him needing minimal respiratory assistance in the form of low-flow oxygen through a nasal cannula.

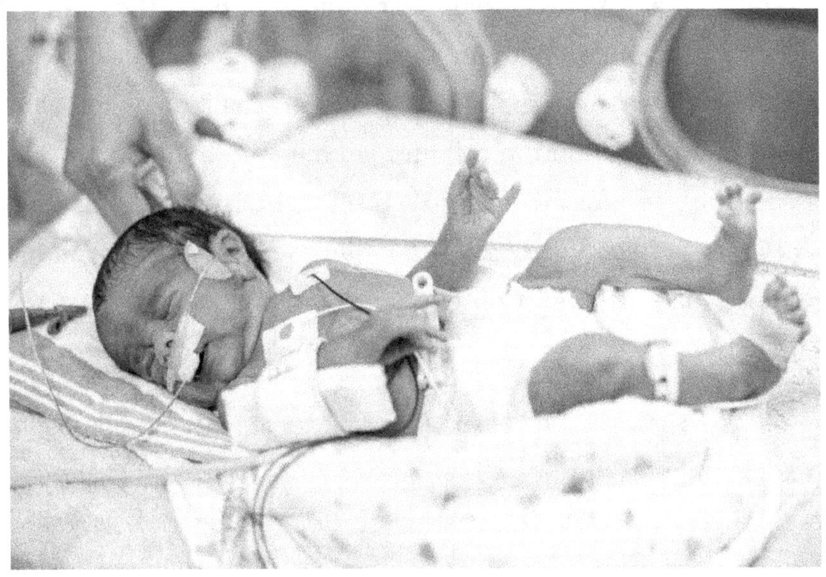

(A baby on nasal cannula)

Low-flow oxygen delivery introduces 100% oxygen in small volume flow. The rationale is that the work of breathing is minimal, and if oxygen is still needed, it can be given while titrating it to the slowest rate of flow. This risk to the eyes due to high oxygen is generally far reduced as, by now, all the blood vessels in the retina are fully developed. The risk of oxygen toxicity to the lungs still persists and will remain an issue to be considered. A trial of a short course of steroids was discussed amongst the team to hasten the process of weaning from oxygen. Dr. Neil felt that it could wait for another couple of weeks as Samson was growing well, and his work of breathing was slow but steadily decreasing.

Thirty-six weeks is a big milestone. Most preterm babies would show some developmental signs, such as attention and better interaction, and their sucking skills improve. This is the time for the medical team to check for any residual damage in the growing brain by ultrasound examination, as well as challenging the baby off respiratory support in a controlled manner. In doing so, they assess the need for low-flow oxygen. This is also when the team considers the administration of immunization against childhood diseases like polio, diphtheria, whooping cough, tetanus, pneumonia, etc.

Samson progressed reasonably well to reach this milestone. He did not need steroids, to the great relief of his parents and the team. His ultrasound examination of the brain did not show any telltale signs suggestive of brain damage. His eyes healed well, and Dr. Brown was happy to follow up with him at nine months of age in his clinic for any further damage to his vision and alignment of the eyes. The respiratory challenge test, otherwise called the Shift test, where the oxygen flow is temporarily discontinued while being monitored closely to see if the baby could tolerate being off for a certain length of time, however, was unsuccessful, indicating that he still needed oxygen. He was, therefore switched from high-flow to low-flow oxygen. Immunizations were administered as his parents readily agreed. This often is a stressful period, mainly because there is always the risk of the need to temporarily increase respiratory support, but thankfully, Samson did not react adversely.

Parents often start preparing for the discharge at this point. Rosy and Rob were excited. Although it was still a few weeks before Samson would be ready for discharge, they stood at the threshold of a new chapter in their lives. Their premature son, Samson, had fought valiantly in the neonatal intensive care unit (NICU), defying the odds day by day. The monitors blinked reassuringly, tracking Samson's tiny breaths and heartbeats. Yet, as the days turned into weeks, a mixture of excitement and trepidation filled their hearts. They were also anxious about the prospect of going home with Samson still needing oxygen. Realizing this, Dr. Neil decided to sit with them and discuss the discharge process and what sort of support and follow-up measures would be put in place.

Dr. Neil sensed their inner turmoil. He sat down with the discharge team, follow-up nurses, the community nurse, Ms. Lorrain, and Rosy and Rob. The room seemed to hold its breath as he explained the discharge process. They discussed the practical aspects—the oxygen tanks, feeding routines, and follow-up appointments. Dr. Neil assured them that a safety net would be woven around Samson, with home nursing visits and a dedicated helpline for any concerns.

As the conversation unfolded, Rosy and Rob felt a glimmer of hope. They were not alone in this journey. The NICU team would continue to be their guiding light, even beyond the hospital walls. Dr. Neil's words echoed in their hearts: "Samson is a fighter, and so are you. Together, we will ensure he thrives." The prospect of taking their fragile bundle home was both exhilarating and nerve-wracking. How would they manage the delicate balance of caring for Samson's medical needs while creating a nurturing environment?

And so, with a mixture of anticipation and gratitude, Rosy and Rob prepared to bring Samson home—a tiny warrior wrapped in love, ready to face the world beyond the NICU.

Discharge Home

The anticipation of bringing their baby home is a powerful source of hope and motivation for parents. Planning for the homecoming, imagining the first night in the nursery, and visualizing life beyond the NICU instill a sense of optimism. This anticipation helps parents stay focused on the positive future ahead.

Contrary to popular belief, discharge planning actually starts from the moment a baby is admitted. However, the practical issues for caring at discharge are discussed as the baby gets closer to their expected date of delivery if the pregnancy had not ended in prematurity. There are several issues to be considered. Basically, the principle involves the same as while in care at the hospital, viz, a scaled-down version of respiratory monitoring and care, nutritional support and monitoring, prevention of infection, and social and emotional support. The discharge planning process brings in a group of professionals, which consists of a discharge planning nurse, the social worker, the community health nurse, the nutritionist, the bio-technician (if the baby is going home with assisted technology in use), the neurodevelopmental therapist and the in-charge physician who could be the same consultant who cared for the baby in the unit or a developmental pediatrician. This group at Waikato Hospital would generally meet every week. A detailed needs assessment was made, and appropriate support was put in place.

It was obvious to the team that Samson would need to go home with oxygen. Arrangements had to be made for continuous oxygen supply. The family had to be taught the process of maintaining constant oxygen delivery and generally the use of monitoring devices such as saturation monitors and the risks of fire that goes with oxygen in the environment, smoking, for instance. The family, particularly the parents, are taught the basic skills of resuscitation. It is of utmost importance that the baby is not exposed to smoke in any form at any stage in his life, more so when he is still recovering from CLD. It is also important to make sure that the house is well-insulated, warm, and dry. The parents and every other person who could or would handle or interact with the family must be made aware of the fragile status of the baby regarding the risk of infection. Although discharge home is a joyous occasion for the family, it can also be a great source of stress. In the case of Rosy and Rob, the fact that they were doctors would help, but it also has the potential to increase their anxiety level, having seen and learned about all the complications from their runs in the NICU and General Pediatrics as students.

The discussion and training for discharge home is a process that can go on for weeks while the team carefully prepares the baby and the family. The parents are encouraged to stay in (room in) and increase their time and involvement in the care of their baby while the neonatal team, in conjunction with the wider discharge planning team, assesses the preparedness of the family and the home situation for the needs of the baby. A follow-up plan is drawn up, and the logistics of the home visits are marked out. The local pharmacy is intimated, and the general practitioner is made aware of the baby's condition in the form of a detailed discharge summary. The lead maternity carer is also informed.

The team had hoped that Samson would be ready in a couple of weeks, but a detailed physical examination revealed that he had developed a hernia through his right inguinal canal. This is not an unusual situation in preterm babies; however, Rosy was very disappointed to learn this. She was well aware of the nature of the hernia and was concerned about the need for another surgery. Hernia is a condition where the content of the bowel extrudes along with all its covering outside the abdominal cavity and bulges under the skin. Besides the obvious mass being visible in the groin, the individual can feel discomfort, but more importantly, the bowel loops could get trapped and obstructed, leading to an emergency called incarceration. This will need urgent attention, hence the concern. Samson was not unduly affected, but Rosy and Rob wanted it sorted before he was discharged. Generally, pediatric surgeons would delay the surgery if possible while carefully monitoring it till the baby is well grown unless a complication, as mentioned, sets in. The risks of postoperative complications are lesser as age advances. Besides, a premature baby with CLD on oxygen has the additional risk of going backward on his respiratory support and occasionally getting back on invasive respiratory support. In such cases, they often advise the baby to be discharged home and bring him back for an elective procedure in a couple of months. It took a bit of discussion and convincing for Samson's parents to agree. Rob was planning to take a few weeks' break from his training when Samson came home to aid with helping Rosy. With further delay, he was concerned that it may come in the way of preparation for his fellowship examination. He finally decided to put that on the back burner in the interest of Samson's health, to everyone's relief. The baby was then discharged home and brought back on a later date for surgery. The operation was done under local anesthesia this time and the baby just needed a day stay. Fortunately, there were no complications, to his parent's great relief.

The days and weeks leading to discharge passed quickly. The nurses arranged for a car seat run. This is a routine procedure to make sure that the family can take the baby home safely in their car. Rob had already arranged for an infant car seat, as advised by the discharge planning team. Arrangements had also been made for an oxygen concentrator (a device to extract oxygen from the atmosphere) and backup oxygen cylinders to be delivered home. All the discharge paperwork was updated, and copies were sent to their family's general practitioner, Dr. Shankar, and medical scripts were sent to the local pharmacy. Samson was eventually discharged home when he was nearing his actual expected date of birth. He weighed just over two and a half kilograms, not exactly thriving but self-feeding satisfactorily. He continued to receive low-flow oxygen from a cannula. Rob had decided to get an apnoea monitor to go with an oxygen saturation monitor supplied by the NICU.

It was an emotional moment for Rosy and Rob. Rosy had arranged for her parents to come in. After months of struggle, watching Samson grow, and grieving the loss of David, here was the moment of truth. Rosy's eyes filled with tears, and Rob's hands trembled. Samson, wrapped in a soft blue blanket, blinked up at them as if he understood the gravity of the moment. Rosy held her breath as the nurses dressed Samson in a onesie that was still too big for him. It was adorned with little elephants—a symbol of strength and resilience. As they wheeled Samson out of the NICU, the hallway felt endless. But every step brought them closer to freedom. The other parents, who had become their companions during late-night feedings, clapped softly as they passed. The nurses waved, their eyes misty with pride. They had seen this scene many times, yet every preterm baby who is discharged home is still a unique experience for these dedicated members of the NICU team. The bond the nursing staff had formed with the family remains tight forever.

With the NICU days behind them, Rosy and Rob realized the enormity of the situation. For them, the journey was just another beginning. They knew it would not be easy, but they were as ready as they could be. Samson had taught them that strength came in the smallest packages and love could move mountains.

With the discharge of a preterm baby from the NICU come many questions not only regarding immediate concerns like risks of infections and readmissions, monitoring for breathing issues like apnoea (cessation of breaths), concerns with nutrition, growth, and development but long-term issues with chronic medical illnesses like asthma, metabolic disease, early onset hypertension, cardiovascular illnesses, diabetes, school performance, earning and learning problems in addition to psychiatric and psychological conditions. Parents do not often think beyond the immediate future at this stage, but it remains the responsibility of the medical staff to follow up with the child in the community, who needs to gradually introduce these concepts. There is a lot of long and very long outcome data now available leading up to old age, but unfortunately, these are not yet well recognized by all healthcare professionals outside the specialty of neonatal medicine and developmental pediatrics. Often, the focused follow-up is limited to the first couple of years of life by these specialists, and the families are then dependent on the family physicians, who are not well equipped at this stage to care for the emerging issues. As such, it becomes the responsibility of the neonatal practitioners to educate the families that the care of a baby born preterm essentially continues life-long.

Neonatal Follow up

The hectic period following the arrival of Samson at home was stressful for Rosy and Rob. They had to readjust to their life again and settle down following the turmoil they had experienced with delivery and the period that followed. Their life had turned upside down. The daily routine of caring for Samson had taken priority, and they both had to postpone their career ambition for an uncertain period. Rosy had three months of paid maternity leave which was now nearing its end. She had to make the choice of returning or taking unpaid leave from training. Her parents were always willing to help, but she felt guilty about relying on her aging parents. She discussed her dilemma with Rob, who had been very helpful throughout but had already decided to return from the two weeks of leave he had taken to help settle Rosy and Samson at home. For most parents, the financial situation had to be considered as well. Often, with a single-person income, it could get tight to run the household. In their mind, however, the uppermost concern was Samson's well-being, and they did not want to compromise. They, therefore, decided that Rosy would take a leave of absence from her position as a trainee for at least six months.

It had taken a while for them to settle into a schedule. They looked forward to the visiting home care nurse who was liaising with Dr. Neil and tweaking down the oxygen flow. Every such reduction came with a period of anxiety as well. It took some time for them to get used to the constant sounds of the oxygen saturation monitors and the occasional false alarms from the apnoea (stoppage of breathing) monitor. The first follow-up visit with Dr. Neil, scheduled for six weeks after discharge, was coming up. Samson was putting on weight steadily and generally looking healthier. He started smiling and interacting with them to the great joy and satisfaction of his parents. By and by, with generous help from her parents, Rosy began to relax and enjoy the process of being a mother.

The visit to the hospital for a review consultation for Samson with Dr. Neil was the next big step for his family. Since returning home, Rosy had not stepped out, and therefore, she was eagerly looking forward to it. The logistics of taking Samson out for his outing from home were not daunting, but careful planning was still needed. Rob had blocked the time from his work in the ward to be present when Rosy brought Samson to the hospital. Rosy's parents had volunteered to drive them in. Rosy wanted the home care nurse to be present as well.

Rosy was feeling relaxed and hoped that Dr. Neil would reinforce everything with the progress achieved so far. When she arrived at the outpatient block, she was met with the home care nurse, who made sure that Samson was safely transferred out of his car seat and taken to the reception. The clerk at the reception, Ms. Rosylin, jumped out of her chair when she saw Rosy with her family. Rosylin was the receptionist at the NICU when Rosy's twins were admitted. She had formed a bond with Rosy and Rob. By then, Rob arrived, and they were ushered into the waiting room. The waiting room was a warm, well-lit, and brightly decorated space for the families and children to sit before being called in for their consultation. It was a common place for all the pediatric specialist's consulting rooms. There were children of all age groups with their parents waiting to see their respective doctors. The nurse in charge of this area takes their weights, length, and head measurements, and clerks are also involved with any specific pre-appointment details identified for individual patients.

Rosy was familiar with this environment, having spent time with pediatric consultants during her run in her internship at the hospital. She wondered, though, how different it felt as a parent. All the memories of her run came flooding in, and she realized how the perspective of an individual changes under different circumstances. Rob, on the other hand, was still thinking about his pending work in the ward. They were shaken out of their reverie when Dr. Neil walked in, calling Samson's name, and greeted them. He quickly checked with them if they were ready to have Samson checked out. They nodded and accompanied him into his chambers. Dr. Neil, after a brief exchange of pleasantries, got about his job. He checked the growth parameters that were entered into Samson's record and nodded as he plotted them on the respective growth curves adjusted for the weeks of prematurity. He informed them that he was really pleased to see the progress on this front. He then requested Rosy to place Samson on the examination table. Meanwhile, he asked if there were any specific concerns regarding Samson's health. As he examined Samson, he kept talking and reassured that Samson was doing very well from the physical examination and developmental point of view. He said he was confident that they would be able to wean him off the Oxygen in the next couple of weeks. He acknowledged the arrival of the home care nurse who had walked in. He then talked to the nurse about how he intends to do that and the monitoring in the form of overnight oxygen saturation runs that he would like to see. Rob remained calm and preoccupied with his thoughts, and when Dr. Neil looked at him, he asked if it was safe for them to remove the apnoea monitor. Dr. Neil said that it was not his recommendation. Anyway, he was confident that Samson was now safely out of the risk period for acute life-threatening events (ALTE). He explained to them that ALTE is one of the immediate concerns that the Neonatal team worries about on discharge home, but studies have shown that the use of apnoea monitors has not reduced the chances of occurrence of these events but it only increases the anxiety of parents because of the false alarms. He then outlined the next steps for them and talked briefly about the need to continue with iron and vitamin supplements till he sees Samson again in about three months' time. He wanted the home care team to continue following Samson till their next visit.

Samson was off Oxygen a few weeks after he was seen at the clinic and continued to thrive. Each of his further visits dealt with specific requirements appropriate for the age, like immunization, the introduction of weaning foods, and what to look for from the developmental point of view. The last visit occurred at two years of age. This is generally believed to be the time period it should take for preterm babies to catch up with their term-born peers in terms of both physical growth and developmental milestones. A formal developmental examination is performed by the specialist team at the one-year mark and at two years to look for any residual delay, and if any delay is noted, appropriate measures to rehabilitate are put in place. Samson did well; he was growing and developing just as well as his peers who were born at term gestation. Fortunately for his parents, no residual delays were identified at this stage in his early life. However, Dr. Neil advised them to be watchful of the various potential issues in the future. These involved all domains of well-being, including learning, language development, physical growth, respiratory, cardiovascular, renal, hypertension, and metabolic diseases like diabetes and hyperlipidemia.

This is the time when most parents, for the first time, wake up to the realities of raising children born prematurely. Their job is not finished yet, and there are so many hurdles still to overcome in the life of a premature baby. For an ideal long-term overall outcome, it is important that the families and the ongoing team are aware of the multitude of problems that still await these babies, as described in the next chapter. The families of preterm babies must be made aware of what needs to be anticipated at every stage in the life of their babies and measures taken in advance to avoid any impediment to their well-being, to achieve the best outcome throughout their lives.

Long-term issues in prematurely born babies

Over the years, the scientific community has woven a tapestry of knowledge, meticulously collecting data on these fragile lives. From the earliest incubators to cutting-edge technology, the survival rates of preterm infants have soared. We have witnessed miracles, but beyond survival lies a deeper quest, which is to ensure the quality of life for these survivors, to enhance survival rates and the richness of life that follows. Yet, within this triumph lies a poignant truth that although most preterm babies do well, not all preterm survivors tread an easy path. Adolescence and adulthood bring their own challenges. Even if initially these individuals appear no different from their full-term born peers, as the years unfold, intellectual and psychiatric struggles, chronic pulmonary issues, metabolic disorders like diabetes and lipid abnormalities, subtle effects of other organ dysfunction, and cardiovascular problems begin to emerge. It is not just their lives that bear the weight. Recent data reveals an unexpected ripple effect due to stress—the shortened lifespan of mothers and parental discord have been reported.

Nearly 10% of the world population (13 to 15 million) are born prematurely every year worldwide. In a small country like New Zealand alone, with a population of just over 5 million, we can expect around 6-7 thousand premature births every year. With the increasing number of extremely premature infants surviving year after year, there is going to be a cumulative increase in the number of survivors. This is going to have a telling effect on the health & well-being of not only the individuals and their families but also on the society and the economies of the nations worldwide.

Fortunately, as mentioned, most preterm-born babies do very well. They can expect to lead a fulfilling and satisfactory life. In fact, in lay literature, we can even see anecdotal reports of miracle babies who have gone on to become geniuses. At the individual level, though, some variability in performance occurs. In reality, however, a long list of problems has been identified amongst the group as a whole. There are many associated factors, both of medical and perinatal nature, in addition to being born prematurely, like the degree of prematurity, low birth weight, brain injury, early neonatal problems, and family/social factors like parental education level, socioeconomic status that affect eventual health and intellectual development. The more immature the individual at birth, the more the risk of long-term problems leading into adulthood

Intellectual disability - this encompasses many domains; prematurity is likely to affect all of them. Prematurity is often associated with the risk of poor motor, cognitive, and linguistic development of the child, as well as behavioral problems that affect, among other areas, the child's performance at school. The rate of extremely preterm (EPT) children who show impairment rates in one or more of these neurodevelopmental domains has been reported to be as high as above 70%. Many of these deficits are mild and not picked up till mid-school age. This slightly lower intellectual performance is more evident in middle childhood when the academic demands of the school level are probably at a higher level. This lower cognitive level may not only have an impact on academic performance but also on other activities of daily living. Poor learners end up being poor earners, which has a ripple effect on future well-being. In this sense, premature birth would pose a risk for the adaptation of these children to different contexts and, finally, for their quality of life.

Psychiatric and psychological problems affect prematurely born babies more than the general population- Some psychiatric disorders do not overtly manifest until adolescence or adulthood, and their consequences can be debilitating. They are associated with an increased risk of a range of severe mental disorders leading into adulthood, including nonaffective psychosis, depressive disorder, bipolar disorders, and increased suicide rates. Studies have shown that they can have increased rates of autism spectrum disorder (ASD), ADHD, Schizophrenia, and mental health issues compared with term-born peers, in addition to elevated rates of anxiety, addiction liability, and mood disorders.

Chronic respiratory problems - Preterm birth is associated with reduced pulmonary function that may persist into early adulthood and is more pronounced in those with a history of CLD or bronchopulmonary dysplasia (BPD). Preterm birth survivors, either with or without BPD, have an increased frequency for the risk of respiratory symptoms commonly reported as asthma and increased bronchodilator use early in life. These outcomes may persist into adulthood and, combined with harmful environmental exposures like air pollution and smoking, may potentially lead to higher risks of chronic obstructive pulmonary disease (COPD) later in adulthood. A large study of a Swedish cohort of persons born in 1973–1979 found that preterm birth was associated with increased mortality attributed to infections (which were predominantly respiratory) at ages 29–36 years. Increased risk of sleep-disordered breathing (SDB) has also been reported.

Cardiovascular morbidity- Epidemiologic studies have consistently linked preterm birth with higher blood pressure in adulthood. Preterm birth is associated with increased risks of ischemic heart disease (IHD) and heart failure in adulthood. These risks were even higher among women, likely due to a lower background incidence of IHD in those born at term compared to men.

Endocrine/Metabolic disorders- Preterm birth has consistently been linked with increased risks of both type 1 and type 2 diabetes later in life and increased risks of lipid disorders and cardiometabolic syndrome in adulthood.

Many other organ systems like the skin, kidneys & immunological systems may also start showing dysfunction in late adolescence and adulthood in these individuals. Increased incidence of early onset of problems related to aging is also emerging as these cohorts begin to enter late adulthood. All these issues also contribute to problems with relationship building. There is a move to recognize premature birth as a chronic condition that requires long-term follow-up to facilitate preventive actions, timely detection, and treatment of adverse health sequelae in adulthood.

A list of recommended follow-ups is included in the appendix for the benefit of families and can be adapted by their family physicians, paediatricians, and adult physicians.

Future of Neonatal-Perinatal Medicine

In the years gone by, we have seen many developments on the research front that have helped improve the survival and quality of life of prematurely born babies. It is only to be expected that future generations of premature babies will do better. Several emerging research trends are not only looking at improved survival and quality of survivors but there is a sincere effort to understand how premature births can be avoided on the one hand and how babies born even before the stage of viability can be managed in an artificial womb on the other. With the ongoing concerns of declining birth rates all over the world, research to improve the survival and quality of babies born at any gestation would hopefully gain momentum.

Traditionally, parents and patients have not been actively involved in shaping research agendas in neonatal medicine. However, recent studies have highlighted the importance of including their perspectives. A Delphi study conducted in Australia and New Zealand involved parents and patients with experience in neonatal care. They identified several research priorities across different life epochs, including parental mental health support, communication between parents and neonatal clinical staff, bonding, and long-term impacts on child health and neurodevelopment.

Researchers continue to make significant strides in monitoring, diagnostics, and therapeutics for neonatal care, starting from the womb, at birth, and during care in the NICU. These technologies offer opportunities for clinical innovation and research. AI and big data analysis are increasingly being applied in neonatal medicine. Just as AI has found applications in various aspects of neonatal care, it is also advancing across pediatric and adult domains. With the development of precision medicine, one can foresee fine-tuning of care of individual babies in the coming years.

The future of neonatal and perinatal care and the whole spectrum of care leading into childhood, adolescence, adulthood, and the elderly is looking bright. Hopefully, with the increasing knowledge and understanding of the lifelong problems prematurely born individuals face, one can expect to see better and individualized care of this emerging group of survivors in the future.

THE END

Appendix

Long-Term Clinical Assessment and Management of Individuals Born Prematurely

	First two years	Preschool 2- 5 years	Early Childhood 5- 10 years	Late Childhood and Adolescent 10 – 19 years	Adulthood
Neonatal F/U General Pead F/U GP F/U	4/6 monthly	Yearly Yearly	As needed* Yearly	As needed* Yearly	As needed*
Medical Issues Growth & Development Organ System Specific	s •/ Δ S/•	s •/ Δ S/•	s •/ Δ S/•	s • S/•	s • S/•
Medical Evaluation Blood Pressure	• s/•/ Δ •/ Δ	• Δ s/•/ Δ	• Δ s/•/ Δ	• Δ s/•/ Δ	• Δ s/•/ Δ

Feeding /Nutrition/Gut	•/ Δ	•/ Δ	Δ	±	±
Lung Function/Asthma	•/ Δ	•/ Δ	±	±	±
Vision & Hearing		•/ Δ	•/ Δ	•/ Δ	•/ Δ
Bone & Blood Health		•/ Δ	•/ Δ	•/ Δ	•/ Δ
Renal/Blood Sugar/Lipid Profile					
Referrals					
Neurodevelopmental	•	±/•	±/•	±/•	±/•
Therapists/Physio/Occupational	•		±/•	±/•	±/•
	±/•		±/•	±/•	±/•
Speech & Language					±/•
Audiology					
Pulmonology					
Cardiology					
Nephrology					

Developmental/ Academic/ Social CDC/Behavior/Psychiatry School/Uni Performance Socialization	•	• ±/•	• • ±/•	• • •	± • •
Disability/Emotional services Home Care Nursing Nutrition & Dietetic	±/• ±/• ±/• ±/•	±/• ±/• ±/•			

Key: S Subjective, by history taking, • to be performed; Δ objective, by a standard testing method; ± need based; * Based on specific medical issues identified

About the Author

Dr. Arun Nair is a retired Neonatal Pediatrician from Waikato Hospital in New Zealand. In a career spanning four decades in various regions of the world, Dr Nair has witnessed and experienced miraculous developments in the field of perinatal medicine in the underdeveloped, developing, and so-called developed world.

His journey began in India, where he received foundational medical education and specialist training in Pediatrics. Earlier in his career, he was among the twenty Pediatricians selected for International Leadership Training in Perinatal Medicine at the University of Illinois, College of Medicine in Chicago, USA. Soon after, he underwent further subspecialty training in Neonatal Intensive Care at Sydney's Westmead Hospital, Australia. Throughout his career, Dr. Nair sought excellence, traveling to renowned centers in his chosen field.

Beyond clinical expertise, Dr. Nair discovered a passion for writing—the science behind life's magic. His previous book, *"Maxim for Living: The Science of Spirituality,"* reflects his unique worldview. In addition to his clinical work with newborn babies, involving extensive reading, research, and teaching, he managed to delve into Philosophy, Neuroscience, and the enigmatic realm of Quantum Mechanics during his spare moments.

His latest work is purposeful: to guide both general readers and medical practitioners from diverse fields through the emotional journey of parents and caregivers. These are the parents of extremely premature babies spending critical time in the Newborn Intensive Care Unit. Dr. Nair also sheds light on long-term issues and the ongoing care necessary for optimal outcomes in premature birth survivors.

Amid declining birth rates, Dr. Nair calls upon global policymakers to allocate resources for the increasing number of vulnerable populations of prematurely born individuals. He envisions this book as an enlightening catalyst, fostering awareness, compassion, and action.